Look what people are saying about talented author Jillian Burns

"With *Let It Ride,* Jillian Burns has written a worderfully steamy, fast-paced story that will keep you turning pages until the very end."
—*Kwips and Kritiques*

"Jillian Burns's latest is an emotionally moving masterpiece with characters whose profound issues create convincing and formidable roadblocks to happiness. The tropical setting will delight. A secondary romance between Kristen's friend and a Hawaiian native is icing on the cake."
—*Affaire de Coeur* on *Once a Hero...*

"Jillian Burns is an author who can take an ordinary, everyday story and make it her own. Burns fans will love this beautifully woven story and new readers will become lifelong fans!"
—*FreshFiction* on *Seduce and Rescue*

Blaze

Dear Reader,

We have exciting news! As I'm sure you've noticed, the Harlequin Blaze books you know and love have a brand-new look, starting this month. And it's *hot!* Don't you agree?

But don't worry—nothing else about the Blaze books has changed. You'll still find those unforgettable love stories with intrepid heroines, hot, hunky heroes and a double dose of sizzle!

Check out this month's red-hot reads....

#729 THE RISK-TAKER by Kira Sinclair
(Uniformly Hot!)

#730 LYING IN BED by Jo Leigh
(The Wrong Bed)

#731 HIS KIND OF TROUBLE by Samantha Hunter
(The Berringers)

#732 ONE MORE KISS by Kathy Garbera

#733 RELENTLESS SEDUCTION by Jillian Burns

#734 THE WEDDING FLING by Meg Maguire

I hope you're as pleased with our new look as we are. Drop by www.Harlequin.com or www.blazeauthors.com to let us know what you think.

Brenda Chin
Senior Editor
Harlequin Blaze

Relentless
Seduction

—

Jillian Burns

HARLEQUIN®
entertain, enrich, inspire™

Recycling programs
for this product may
not exist in your area.

ISBN-13: 978-0-373-79737-0

RELELNTLESS SEDUCTION

www.Harlequin.com

Printed in U.S.A.

ABOUT THE AUTHOR

Jillian Burns has always read romance, and spent her teens immersed in the worlds of Jane Eyre and Elizabeth Bennett. She lives in Texas with her husband of twenty years and their three active kids. Jillian likes to think her emotional nature—sometimes referred to as *moodiness*—has found the perfect outlet in writing stories filled with passion and romance. She believes romance novels have the power to change lives with their message of eternal love and hope.

Books by Jillian Burns

HARLEQUIN BLAZE
466—LET IT RIDE
572—SEDUCE AND RESCUE
602—PRIMAL CALLING
670—ONCE A HERO

To get the inside scoop on Harlequin Blaze and its talented writers, be sure to check out blazeauthors.com.

Other titles by this author available in ebook format.
Don't miss any of our special offers. Write to us at the following address for information on our newest releases.

Harlequin Reader Service
U.S.: 3010 Walden Ave., P.O. Box 1325, Buffalo, NY 14269
Canadian: P.O. Box 609, Fort Erie, Ont. L2A 5X3

This is for Alice, a dear friend,
who was the first one to believe I could actually
write a novel, and made it seem like more than
a pipe dream when she gave me
"How to Write a Romance Novel."

And for my mama,
who is always there for me, no matter what.

As usual, it takes a village to raise a romance novel.
Thank you to Charlaine Harris and her vampire bar,
Fangtasia, for my inspiration. Thank you to
dear friend and author extraordinaire Von for the
plotting help, and to my amazing critique partners,
Pam and Linda, for making sure my characters
have believable motivations. And to my editor,
Kathryn Lye, for her amazing patience.

1

CLAIRE BROOKS HESITATED at the door to Once Bitten. A sense of eerie foreboding made her shiver.

Nonsense. She'd read too many gothic novels in her youthful summer days.

There was no such thing as premonition, and it certainly couldn't make one shiver. It was merely the cold, drizzly night. And her worry for Julia.

Despite the jazzy wail from a street musician's trumpet down the street, the occasional *clip-clop* of horses' hooves pulling carriages, and tourists still roaming the sidewalks, this area didn't feel as if it was part of the French Quarter.

It was simply another New Orleans bar, the only difference being it attracted tourists with its singularly macabre theme. More importantly, it was the only clue she had.

Claire pushed the button on her phone and compared the picture Julia had sent her last night to the purple neon sign in front of her. Last night, Julia had been standing in this exact spot. So this was the logical place to begin her search.

That picture was the last communication she'd had from Julia. Despite leaving her dozens of increasingly frantic messages, Claire had heard nothing from her friend in almost twenty-four hours. What if she was already…dead?

She shook off the horrifying thought, swung open the door and stepped purposefully inside.

Creepy discordant music assaulted her ears. Her eyes stung and her nostrils itched from the smoky incense. But at least the temperature inside was warmer than the chilly rain outside.

She closed her umbrella, shrunk it to its mini size and placed it in her oversize tote bag. Searching for Julia's mischievous smile and blond hair, Claire began to study the assortment of unique individuals gyrating around the dance floor—or in iron cages hanging from the ceiling.

In addition to people with multiple piercings, an overabundance of tattoos and unusual costumes, there was a man wearing only tight, black shorts and a leather collar around his neck. And working her way around the room was a naked woman with a large, very much alive snake wrapped around her torso. A large percentage of the patrons sported dyed-black hair, kohl-lined eyes and…fangs.

Whether they were fake, or real incisors filed to a

point, the fangs didn't disturb Claire. There was no such thing as vampires. But these people were all welcome to their eccentricities. The only thing Claire cared about was finding Julia. And if it meant questioning every vampire wannabe in this place then that's what she'd do.

She lifted her chin and joined the occupants of the famous vampire bar, Once Bitten.

As she tried to make her way through the mob of sweaty people, she felt their stares on her as if she were the weird one. Actually, she guessed she was.

But she kept mingling, searching faces for Julia or the guy she'd disappeared with. Eventually she found herself in a darkened lounge with low, red velvet sofas forming an enclosed sitting area. Between each grouping of seats lay old-fashioned wooden coffins, on which people had placed their drinks. Coffins as coffee tables. Claire raised her brow. Clever.

These sitting areas were occupied with similar-looking patrons. Goths, freaks and vampires.

But no Julia.

A glance to her right revealed a surprisingly normal-looking bar with neon beer advertisements flashing above a mirrored wall stacked with shot glasses and bottles of liquor. Cocktail glasses hung upside down from a rack above the bar with more patrons perched on black wooden stools.

She headed there, pulling out her cell phone and bringing up the picture of Julia on the way. Snagging a lone stool, she leaned forward against the scratched, worn oak to catch the bartender's attention.

He was wiping a tumbler with a pristine white towel, while at the same time conducting a flirtatious discussion with two coeds in low-riding blue jeans and halter tops. The girls were engrossed in whatever he was saying, and who could blame them when he wore such a dangerously sinful grin.

She summoned her inner Julia and raised her hand and waved. "Excuse me?"

The moment the man turned her way a quiver of desire shot through her. Slate-gray eyes fringed with dark lashes bore into her, freezing her in place. His collar-length black hair wasn't dyed, nor was the thick stubble darkening his angular jaw.

His grin softened as he leisurely replaced the tumbler on a shelf behind him before sauntering over to flatten his palms on the bar before her.

"What you need, *cher?*" His voice was as smooth and as deeply Southern as Spanish moss hanging from a Cypress tree. He wore a wide leather bracelet on his left wrist and a thick onyx ring—a bat with its wings wrapped around his right ring finger. She lifted her gaze to his hard chest outlined by a tight black tee.

Claire opened her mouth but nothing came out. "Have y-y—" She felt her face heat and her throat close up as he stared at her expectantly. Two decades of therapy and determination to overcome her stutter destroyed in an instant of anxiety.

Anxiety for her friend, of course. This breathlessness was in no way attributable to the proximity and attention of the bartender. The only true friend she had was missing. It was natural to be distraught.

Remembering her purpose, Claire drew in a calming breath, lifted her phone to the bartender's eye level and clicked the button to bring up Julia's picture again. "Have you seen this woman in your bar tonight?

The bartender's gaze shifted down to her phone and back to her eyes without the rest of him moving a muscle. "No."

"But you r-recognize her? She was here l-last night."

He moved his weight from one foot to the other, causing his hips to shift, as well. "*Cher,* I've got hundreds of customers coming through here."

Claire gritted her teeth, biting back a stinging rebuke. "Please." She shifted her phone in front of his nose. "She's missing and I have to find her."

A muscle in his jaw twitched. "If she's missing, call the cops." He turned away.

As if she hadn't already tried the police first thing this morning. Julia was an adult, they'd said. Must be missing for forty-eight hours, they'd said. They hadn't taken Claire's fear for her friend seriously at all. As if Claire didn't know when something was really wrong with Julia.

She'd known Julia since third grade and Claire knew without a doubt that this was not just a case of Mardi Gras hangover. Sure, Julia had ditched her last night to hook up with that weirdo with the tattoo. Claire was accustomed to Julia's free-spirited ways. Even when she hadn't returned to their hotel room by this morning, Claire had calmly packed their things and gone to the airport, assuming Julia would come racing up to her at the last minute, full of false chagrin and a scintillating account of her adventures with the "vampire."

But she hadn't.

And Claire wasn't leaving New Orleans without making sure Julia was alive and well.

"She might've been with a guy who had three blood drops t-tattooed down the corner of his mouth," Claire called after the bartender.

The bartender froze, and several people at the bar around her quieted and stared at her. He turned back and leaned in close, conspiratorially. At last, she would gain some useful information. She leaned forward and caught a hint of his spicy intoxicating cologne.

"This is a vampire bar. Lots of people have that tattoo."

Hope deflated. And irritation flared. He was taunting her. Then understanding dawned. She yanked her purse open, pulled out a twenty-dollar bill and slipped it across the bar toward him. "Perhaps this will help you r-remember the man or my friend?"

His eyes narrowed and his lips tightened, harsh and cynical. "You want a drink, I'm your man. Otherwise, I can't help you." He gave his attention to the waitress who'd stepped up with an order.

Claire fumed. "I'll have a strawberry d-daiquiri," she called out.

He glanced at her, brows raised. "A strawber—" His lips curved up at the corners. "Coming right up." As he shook the hair from his wary eyes, a tiny silver loop in his left ear gleamed in the light.

He moved gracefully, spinning back and forth, grabbing bottles and pouring alcohol, and drawing beer into mugs with speed and precision. Tall, but slim, except for his wide shoulders and large biceps, he could've been a member of the Boston rowing club. Yet, unlike those privileged boys, this man seemed unaware of his masculine good looks.

Finally, the waitress left with her filled tray. Then he bent to lift a clear plastic bowl from under the bar.

Her gaze shot straight to his behind and the worn jeans outlining his impossibly sexy derriere. Wait. Was she actually checking out a man's bottom? In her twenty-eight years as a female, she'd never understood why other women noticed things like that. But, now, now that her best friend was missing and possibly in danger, *now* she…noticed?

He peeled off the lid, grabbed a handful of large, red-ripe strawberries and dropped them into a blender. As he prepared her drink, he stole a strawberry from the bowl and popped it into his mouth. He glanced at her and she looked away, feeling her cheeks heat with embarrassment.

She should be searching the bar for her friend or that

guy, showing Julia's picture around. Claire spun, putting her back to the bar, and scanned the room.

"Here you go."

She jumped and turned back as he set the fruity drink in front of her and took the twenty still lying on the bar. He sauntered over to a computer, touched the screen and made change when a drawer popped open.

Digging a business card from her purse, she scribbled her hotel's name and her cell number on it and shoved it into his hand as he offered her the change.

"Please. Keep the change and if you see my friend, would you call me? My cell's on here and where I'm staying—the Les Chambres R-Royale."

Before he could refuse, she snatched up her drink and plunged into the crowd.

His fingers had been hot and rough. Claire swallowed back the tingle she'd felt at the brief contact.

Bringing up the picture of Julia, she began stopping each person and asking if they'd seen her friend. Someone here had to have seen Julia last night. Or that creep she'd left with during the Mardi Gras parade. It wasn't even eleven yet. The night was young.

Rafe watched the woman stop his patrons one by one and show them the picture on her phone. That couldn't be good for business. Yet he couldn't bring himself to throw her out. Her big brown eyes behind the thick lenses had sparked with intelligence, and...authentic concern.

Not your problem, Moreau.

He eyed the card she'd forced on him, debating whether to pitch it in the circular filing cabinet.

Dr. Claire Brooks, PhD
Senior Scientist/Group Leader
Cell Line Generation
Cambridge, Mass
555-496-4949

Doctor? He whistled. What the hell was cell line generation?

He glanced at her again. She was still grilling his customers.

Boy, was she out of her element. The frizzy chestnut hair and decades out of style clothing couldn't have stood out more if she'd been dressed like a nun. All it would take was her asking the wrong person... Plus she was corrupting the vibe. Tourists came here to enter a different world, and the freaks and true believers came here to get their crazy on.

If he looked up the word *sensible,* there'd probably be a picture of this woman. And yet. She'd braved this place to look for her friend.

As he watched she stopped one of his regulars, a die-hard vamp who had the three blood drops tattooed down the corner of his mouth. The guy tried to brush her away, but she moved to block his path.

He scowled and shoved her into another dude Rafe

didn't recognize and her drink splashed down the front of his T-shirt. The fact he was wearing a collar with sharp metal spikes was not a good sign. Dog Collar Guy grabbed her by the throat, his face inches from hers, his teeth bared.

Her eyes widened and filled with fear.

Damn it. Rafe leaped around the bar, shoved his way to the altercation and inserted himself between the collar-man and the good doctor.

"What the—?"

Rafe got in his face. "You lay hands on a customer of mine again, you'll leave in an ambulance," he snarled. "Now get out."

The psycho hesitated and Rafe signaled his bouncer, Bulldog.

Why the hell he hadn't let Bulldog handle it from the beginning he had no clue. Collar-man saw Bulldog headed toward them and raised his hands. "Okay, okay." He made a beeline for the door.

The woman began coughing when collar-man released her. "Thank y—"

Rafe gripped her arm and dragged her toward the door.

"What are you d-doing?" She struggled, but she was no match for him. "Let go of me."

"You're disturbing my customers." Once outside, he whistled for a cab down the street and tugged her to the curb as it pulled up. "Les Chambres Royale," he bent to inform the cabbie, and then opened the back door for her.

"I'm not l-leaving without some information." She managed to fold her arms over nice-size curves that had been hidden before by her crocheted...whatever she called that thing. At the same time, she hitched her huge purse up onto her shoulder and pushed her eyeglasses higher on her nose. Why did he find that appealing?

"Look, this isn't the kind of place you want to be hanging around."

She rolled her shoulders and lifted her chin. "I'm staying here to find my friend."

"It's my bar and I say you're not."

"Hey, is someone getting in or what?" the cabbie yelled out the window.

Rafe leaned in the front window. "Start the meter." When he looked back at the woman, she was biting her thumbnail and he could've sworn he saw the wheels and cogs turning as a plan formed.

"If you don't let me inside, I swear I'll come back every night, stand outside your d-door and ask every-one before they enter—"

"Okay, okay." Damn it. "If I say I'll see what I can find out, will you get in the damn cab?"

She smiled and Rafe blinked. When she smiled it changed her entire face. Softened it. Brightened it. "You promise? You want Julia's picture? I can make copies. I'll b-bring them tomorrow."

He took her elbow and guided her into the backseat

of the cab. "Don't come here. I'll call you if I learn anything." He slammed the door and bent at the waist to look her in the eyes. "Just don't get your hopes up."

She scowled and might have responded, but the cab pulled away.

As Rafe watched the checkered cab disappear into the mist of the chilly night, the back of his neck itched. After a lifetime of getting into it, scheming to get out of it and learning to avoid it, he knew trouble when he saw it.

And that woman was going to be trouble.

2

THE NEXT NIGHT CLAIRE slipped unobtrusively onto a low red velvet sofa in the back of Once Bitten and scanned the crowd around her.

No sign of Julia tonight, either. Or the guy she'd taken off with.

Panic was invading Claire's psyche like the bacteria she studied under a microscope. Experimenting with different cell lines for the production of recombinant molecules seemed like child's play compared to dealing with this mess. In fact, she'd conference-called her team back in Boston this morning to check on their latest cell culture development, and it seemed they were doing just fine without her.

That had been somewhat…disconcerting.

Then she'd placed a call to her mother and father to update them on her progress in finding Julia. At least they took her concerns seriously. Unlike the police force here.

She'd waited around the French Quarter station almost two hours this morning before a detective finally spoke with her. Of course, he'd told her the same thing the officer had told her yesterday. It was Mardi Gras, lots of people go missing and show up a couple of days later, hung over, and with a great story to tell their grandkids, etc.

Officially, Julia wouldn't be considered missing until tomorrow morning when she'd been gone for forty-eight hours. And Claire had looked up the statistics. The chances of finding someone *after* the first forty-eight hours lowered dramatically. Anything could've happened to her by now.

It was obvious Claire couldn't wait for the police.

A familiar ball of frustration roiled in her stomach and she clenched her fists. If only she hadn't agreed to go to Mardi Gras with Julia.

No. If she'd refused to accompany her friend on this trip, Julia would've just gone to New Orleans alone. And then no one would've even known she'd disappeared.

Julia was impulsive, and even sometimes foolish, but she would never just take off without eventually checking in. Something was wrong. And she had to find her friend before it was—statistically speaking—too late.

Worst case scenarios kept flashing through her mind. Julia robbed and beaten. Or maybe that guy she'd gone off with had drugged and raped her. Maybe she'd been left for dead in some alley. Or kidnapped and sold into white slavery—

Okay. Maybe that was just too far. The best way to help her best friend was to remain calm and breathe deeply. She resumed scanning the crowds for Julia.

"You the one caused the trouble here last night?"

Claire shifted on the sofa and her vision was blocked by a silky, floor-length black dress molded to a petite frame from ankle to bosom. The woman's jet-black hair was spiked out on the left side of her head and shaved bald on the right. She had so many piercings, rings and studs through her lip, brows, nose and ears, that Claire couldn't count them all.

"Listen." The woman crouched before her, bringing their eyes level. "We don't need no trouble in this place." She poked her finger at Claire. "I saw your friend here the other night and she was fine when she left. That's all you need to know about Once Bitten. So you should get your big ol' a—"

"It's okay, Ro. I'll handle this." The bartender from the night before spoke from behind Claire.

Startled, Claire jerked around and fell off the sofa, landing on her butt. Oh, geez. Maybe she could just crawl into one of these coffins.

The woman, Ro, straightened, slapped her hands on her slim hips and flattened her lips at the bartender. Then with a shrug of one shoulder, she sauntered off.

"You all right?" He bent to take her elbow and helped pull her to her feet. She could hear the smirk in his tone.

"Fine. I'm fine." Her face felt on fire and she couldn't look at him as she brushed off her corduroys.

"I thought I told you not to come back here."

The back of her neck tingled as she felt his stare on her. She knew what he saw. A frumpy, frizzy-haired, nerd-head. And he was impossibly handsome with his perfectly unshaven jaw and his tousled dark hair and his intense gray eyes.

What did it matter? She was here to find Julia.

"Come with me." He grasped her arm and tugged her along behind him to the bar, confident that she would obey. She almost yanked out of his hold, but he might have information for her.

"Drink this." He grabbed a shot glass and filled it with brown liquid from a bottle that read, "Wild Turkey."

"I don't need whiskey."

"It's bourbon. And you definitely look like you need it."

Claire took the glass and brought it cautiously to her lips. Then she glanced at the bartender.

He folded his arms over his chest. "If I wanted you gone, I wouldn't need to drug you. I could just throw you out like I did last night."

True. But she still didn't trust him. She took a careful sip. Fire. Burning the back of her throat, all the way down to her stomach. She gasped, grabbed her throat and glared at him.

"It gets better. Take another sip."

She *was* feeling less tense, so she sipped again. "Mmm." She nodded her agreement.

He raised a smug brow. "What are you doing here?"

"You said you'd call."

He shook his hair away from his eyes. "I said I'd let you know if I learned anything."

"I'm not disrupting your bar. I'm just watching to see if Julia or that guy comes in."

"And then what?"

"What?"

"What'll you do if the guy does show up? You think you can appeal to his sense of honor and he'll just confess to whatever it is he did with your friend?"

Her stomach tightened as his soft Southern accent contrasted sharply with images of Julia fighting for her life, being tied up and throw in a trunk, injured or… dead. "Well, I'll—I'll call the police and tell them to bring him in for questioning."

"And what if he says he left her alive and well the other night?"

She folded her arms, mimicking him. "Whose side are you on?"

"I'm on my own side. I don't want another scene in my bar."

"Fine. Then I'll question him once he leaves *your* bar."

He shook his head. "You got a death wish, *cher?*"

Cher? The Cajun shorthand for *cherie?* Darling in French. Something in her stomach fluttered and tingled. No one had ever called her darling before. Not that he meant it as an endearment. He didn't even know her. He probably called every woman that so he wouldn't have to remember her name the next morning.

She straightened her spine. "My name is Claire." She offered her right hand. "Claire Brooks. And you are?"

One corner of his mouth curled up. "You gave me your card last night, Doctor, remember?"

"Oh." She could feel her face heating again. Another dorky move. But what was new? She kept her hand extended, and…he took it.

"Rafe Moreau."

She smiled. So silly to be happy over a handshake. "Mr. Moreau."

"Rafe will do." His hand enveloped hers in warmth. Her hands were always so cold, it felt wonderful, the heat, the roughness of his palm and the wave of awareness that swept over her. Skin touching skin. His very maleness so close to her, exuding some sort of sexual heat.

She snatched her hand away.

He probably wasn't even conscious of how sexy he was.

"Listen, Claire. Why don't you go back—"

She gasped.

"What?"

Ignoring Rafe, Claire shoved away from the bar and strode across the lounge area. She stepped in front of a punked-out bleached blonde. "Where did you get that?" Claire pointed to the necklace draped over the blonde's black leather bustier. Hanging from a thick silver chain was a pewter pentacle about two inches in diameter.

She screwed up her face in a look of disgust and turned away. "None of your business."

Claire grabbed her arm. She'd finally found a lead to Julia and she wasn't about to lose it. "It most certainly is my business. I know for a fact that necklace couldn't possibly belong to you."

The woman yanked her arm from Claire's grasp. "You don't know nuthin'. Now, get out of my face before I—"

"Is there a problem here?" Rafe appeared beside Claire and stepped between them.

"Yeah, this bitch is bothering me."

"Rafe. That necklace." Claire pointed to the jewelry on the chain. "It belongs to Julia. She would never part with it willingly."

Rafe glanced from Claire to the necklace, then back to Claire. "How can you be sure?"

Claire narrowed her eyes at the woman. "Maybe I should just call the police and let them look into it."

"Man, she's crazy. I'm outta here." The woman spun to leave, but Rafe clutched her shoulder.

"This will just take a sec." He stared at the woman and whatever she saw in his expression convinced her to wait. Nice talent to have.

The bleached blonde shrugged. "Whatever."

Rafe looked back at Claire.

"I gave it to Julia for her graduation from Cosmetology School. It's engraved on the back. My name and her name and the date, 5-27-04."

Rafe raised his brows and turned toward the bustiered woman. "Free drinks the rest of the night if you let me see the back of your necklace."

The woman's eyes widened. "Sure!" She wrenched the chain up and over her head and dropped it in his waiting palm.

Rafe turned it over and Claire leaned in to look.

As she'd known it would be, there on the back was the engraving that proved it was Julia's.

"I TOLD YOU!" Dr. Claire Brooks tried to snatch the necklace from him, but Rafe was quicker, dodging her grasp.

Undeterred, the stubborn woman gave her attention to the blonde. "Where did you get this?"

The blonde sniffed. "Why should I tell you?"

"I could pay you."

Whoa. Rafe almost warned the good doctor against offering money, but hey, he'd done enough already.

Blondie hesitated. "Yeah? How much?"

The doctor's brow crinkled and she lifted her huge purse to her chest, dug around inside it and finally produced a couple of bills. "Would you take twenty dollars?"

"Make it fifty."

Heh. Blondie was no fool.

"I'll give you seventy-five," the doctor shot back,

pushing her glasses up on her nose. "For the information *and* the necklace."

The blonde's eyes glittered with greed. "I got it at the Blue Bayou Flea Market." She held her palm out expectantly.

The naive doctor set her chin. "Which stall?"

The blonde pursed her lips and scowled. "I don't know! Hey, are you gonna pay me or what?"

Dr. Brooks turned her back, hunched over and pulled something out from the neckline of her shirt. Turning back around, she slapped the money into Blondie's waiting hand, who made a beeline for the bar.

Shaking his head, Rafe handed the necklace to the doctor. "You paid way too much for that, *cher*."

She shrugged. "I didn't want to cause another disturbance in your bar."

Rafe blinked. Had she truly been worried about his business? Right. She probably just didn't want to get thrown out again.

"Well, thank you for your help." She extended her hand. "Offering that woman free drinks all night was extremely generous of you."

Rafe stared at her right hand. He should shake it and get her out of his life forever. "Tell the police. Let them check it out."

She dropped her hand. "Of course, I'll tell them."

Good.

"But I also intend to search the flea market myself."

Of course she did. He shook his head.

"If it's anything like the flea markets back home in Missouri, this place will have hundreds of stalls. I doubt the N.O.P.D. will have the manpower to question each one of the proprietors."

Rafe shrugged. He didn't need to get any more involved.

She placed her hand on his forearm and he tensed reflexively. "Really, thank you." Her lips curved in a small smile before she turned toward the front door.

"Hey," he called after her. When she looked back he folded his arms across his chest, trying to ignore the uneasy feeling in his gut. "Don't stay out after dark."

She frowned. "I can take care of myself." Her expression became smug. "I have my trusty can of pepper spray."

Pepper spray? She thought that would deter a gang during a turf war or stop a junkie jonesing for a hit? Damn it, what did he care what this woman did? He stared after her as she walked out of his bar and his life. Good riddance. He didn't need her causing him any more trouble.

He went back to his bartending and didn't give her another thought the rest of the night. Except for the times he glanced down at the tub of strawberries. Or when he had to pour Blondie another free drink. Or when the front door would open and he'd look over expecting to see her walking back in.

He cursed under his breath long and low the third

time he caught himself feeling vaguely disappointed when it wasn't her. What was wrong with him?

About four o'clock he locked the door behind the last straggling customers and headed for his office in the back.

Ro was lounging on his sofa, already changed into jeans and a tank top. "Free drinks, Rafe? All night?" She scowled and pursed her lips. "That's your idea of handling it?"

"My bar." He plunked down in his chair, pulled the bank bag out of the desk drawer and stuffed all the cash from the night's take into it. He'd count it later.

"It's just that I've never seen you take on a charity case before."

"It's not charity." What was Ro's problem, anyway? "I got her out of here with the least amount of commotion. Commotion is bad for business."

Ro looked suspicious. "So, is she gone for good now?"

"Yep." But something told him the doctor's situation wasn't going to be so easily solved.

"So…you want to…" Ro dangled her leg off the edge of the sofa. "Let off a little steam?"

Normally, he might have taken her up on her offer. "Nah, I better get the accounts payable since it's almost the end of the month." He opened his accounts book and grabbed a pencil.

Ro blinked, and then got to her feet. "Sure. Some other time, maybe." She sauntered to the door, opened it and then turned back. "I got a bad feeling about that strange woman, Rafe." He looked up at her and she seemed genuinely worried. Then she stepped out and closed the door behind her.

Rafe studied the spot where she'd stood for a moment, ran a hand over his jaw and then turned back to his desk. He worked the books for half an hour, but he couldn't concentrate. He was restless. Something did feel wrong, but he couldn't place what.

Disgusted with himself, he slammed his accounting book closed and trudged upstairs to his tiny apartment. He rubbed his stomach, trying to ignore that hollow pit feeling he always got when the shit was about to hit the fan. The way it always did, sooner or later.

Things were going pretty well with his bar right now though.

For seven long years he'd worked like a dog on offshore rigs in the Gulf to save enough to buy his own place. Then, it'd taken months to find real estate he could afford in the perfect location for his bar. And after signing the papers for this place, he'd overseen a complete remodel, spending six months getting it decked out just the way he wanted it.

The old man had drummed into him night after drunken night that he'd never be worth anything. Turning a profit on this place had been a big "Screw you, you old bastard!" to the man who'd raised him from the age of twelve. And though his pappy had been long dead, it'd still felt good.

By the time Rafe stepped out of the shower and got in bed, the sun was almost up. He laced his fingers behind his head and stared at a spot on the ceiling. He'd done what he'd set out to do. He'd proved his pappy wrong. He had everything he wanted. So, naturally, something was about to take it all away. Story of his life.

That's what was bugging him. Things had been going too well lately. And now some tourist had disappeared from *his* bar.

Oh, the cops would love that. They'd finally get that no-good, juvie, banger Rafe Moreau and lock him away where he belonged.

All because of that woman. Dr. Claire Brooks.

He'd known she was nothing but trouble.

At least she hadn't pushed the cops on him yet.

But the last thought he remembered having before he fell asleep was what would the good doctor look like without her glasses?

3

"THE BLUE BAYOU FLEA MARKET, please," Claire informed the cab driver after sliding into his backseat. As the cab pulled away from the police station, her stomach growled, but she hadn't been able to eat this morning. Fear, anxiety and dread all churned inside her, and food would only have added nausea to the mix.

She'd gone to the police station first thing this morning. Now that it had been officially forty-eight hours since Julia had gone missing, Claire had hoped to be taken more seriously. But the desk sergeant hadn't seemed particularly interested in her information about the necklace and the flea market.

He'd acted as if he still believed Julia was merely holed up somewhere with a Mardi Gras lover and would show up soon. At least he'd opened a case file and taken down all her information, Julia's cell number, printed up her DMV picture and promised they'd check out the flea market. They even sent her to a sketch artist to describe the guy Julia had left the parade with, and put an APB out with the artist's rendering.

Claire hadn't mentioned Once Bitten. She wasn't sure exactly why not, except Rafe had gone above and beyond helping her deal with that woman who'd had Julia's necklace. If he'd had anything to do with Julia's disappearance, would he have helped her like that? Or was she letting his masculine appeal blind her to any signs of guilt? When she was around him, she had difficulty concentrating. He made her...flustered and self-conscious.

But that was no reason not to be thorough. She owed it to Julia to do whatever it took to find her and save her. Just as Julia had saved Claire so long ago.

After checking with the cab driver to ask if he'd come back when the flea market closed, she paid him a generous tip from her fast disappearing emergency cash.

After tonight, she'd need to make arrangements for alternative accommodations. One of the most historic hotels in New Orleans, Les Chambres Royale wasn't exactly the most frugal of lodgings. But she'd hated to leave the hotel in case Julia showed up. Claire had even requested the same room after returning from the airport in the hope that Julia still had her key. She'd been surprised the hotel still used the old-fashioned brass keys, but now Claire was glad. Maybe Julia was in their room right this minute....

The hotel knew to call her cell if Julia came back.

With a sigh, Claire headed for the first stall she saw. Who knew? Maybe she'd get lucky and hit the first person she asked.

Five hours later, Claire felt the urge to kick herself for being so naive.

She'd systematically approached each flea market stall beginning with the southwest corner and traveling north along a row and back south down the next, working her way steadily east. At every establishment she would produce the necklace, the picture of Julia and describe the guy with the blood drops tattoo.

No one had seen Julia or the necklace or the guy. To make matters worse it had begun drizzling a half hour ago and despite her trusty umbrella, Claire was bedraggled and shivering from the icy dampness. She didn't even want to think about what her hair must look like in this moisture. Frankenstein's bride had nothing on her when it came to frizz. But none of that would've mattered if she'd found whoever sold Julia's necklace.

The rain finally stopped. She folded up her umbrella, took off her glasses and cleaned them with a piece of tissue from her tote. She needed to regroup. The aroma of Cajun spices drifted around her and her protesting stomach finally forced her to stop at a vendor.

Crawfish etouffe, shrimp gumbo and several varieties of jambalaya made Claire's stomach growl and her mouth water. She chose a bowl of jambalaya with chicken and sausage and sat to savor the Southern flavors with a large chunk of French bread.

Her first bite made her moan in pleasure. She could learn to love a place that produced food like this. The people down here took polite to a whole new level and, despite the daily afternoon drizzle, the air held a soft fragrance that Boston could never match. A heady fusion of magnolias, even when not in bloom, and the earthy scent of mud from the Mississippi flowing along the city's border.

With a wistful sigh, she threw her empty Styrofoam bowl and plastic spoon into the trash, wiped her hands and mouth with the travel-size wet-wipes from her tote, and trudged back to the row of booths where she'd left off.

The sun was setting and Claire only had one row of booths left to question. Almost on autopilot, she held out the necklace to the elderly lady sitting in a folding chair behind a card table. "Did you sell this necklace?" The crocheted doilies and afghans on display didn't give Claire much hope.

The old lady's face transformed into a mask of suspicion. "Why do you want to know?"

Claire's heart tripped and then raced to a double beat. "It belongs to a friend of mine. Where did you get it? Who gave it to you? Was it this woman?" She pulled up the picture of Julia on her phone.

"Nah, I was doin' a favor for my grandson. He asked me to sell it."

"Y-your grandson? Does he have three blood drops tattooed down the left corner of his mouth?"

The lady scrunched up her face. "Heavens, no. He's a good boy. Not like that Shadow." Straightening, her eyes widened in fear. "Oh, lordy, you ain't the police, are you? He'll hurt me for sure for telling you."

"No." Claire shook her head. "No, not the police. Do you know where I can find…Shadow?"

Her eyes narrowed again. "No. And I don't want to."

Claire let out a breath. The woman clearly suspected her. "Would your son maybe have mentioned where Shadow hangs out or where he works?"

The woman guffawed. "He don't work." She shook her head derisively.

Claire squeezed the pentacle in her fist until it dug into her flesh, sharp and painful. She was too close to give up now. Her best strategy was the truth. "Ma'am, the fact is my best friend went off with Shadow a couple of days ago and I haven't seen her since and I'm worried something happened to her. I need to find Shadow and ask him before—" How embarrassing. Her voice caught and her lip trembled.

"Hush, child." The old lady stood and came around the table to put her arm around Claire. "I'll tell you what I know, never you mind the tears." She leaned close to Claire's ear. "That Shadow is no good. I told my boy not to hang around that trash, but he keeps coming around. Wanting me to sell stuff for him."

She leaned close and cupped a hand around her mouth. "Uses the money for drugs, I'm sure. But he scares me so I don't tell him no. One time I heard him trying to get my boy to go to this bar with him. What was the name…?" She tapped a finger to her lips. "Something about caves or holes or… I remember it sounded disgustin'…" She snapped her fingers. "The Pit!"

Claire nodded, surreptitiously wiping a tear from her cheek. "O-okay, thank you so much for your help." She bought a set of doily coasters from her, thanked her again and then headed for the entrance to look for her cab.

Her mind was working rapid-fire, deciding what to do next. Go to that bar, see if this Shadow guy would even show up there and— And what? Call the police? Maybe Julia would be at The Pit with him. Claire's breathing hitched. She almost hoped Julia wouldn't be there with this Shadow person.

It was almost dark. Stalls were closing up. She stood alone in the parking lot. The place had been crowded earlier. She shivered as the hairs on her arms stood out. She glanced to her right and left, feeling someone's eyes on her.

That was absurd. No one knew she was here.

Except Rafe Moreau.

CLAIRE WHISPERED A SHORT prayer of thanks when she saw the cab pull into the flea market parking lot. She was more than a little spooked. Chiding herself that she was letting her imagination run wild didn't help.

She'd never really thought of herself as having much of an imagination.

Digging into her purse, Claire pulled out her cell phone and the card the sergeant in charge of Julia's case had given her. She dialed his number and his brusque, "Mulroney," calmed her fears slightly. She told him what she'd learned about "Shadow" and that he might be hanging out at a bar called The Pit.

Mulroney promised he'd send an officer to check it out, but his tone still suggested they were being sent on a wild goose chase.

If that was Mulroney's attitude, she probably ought to check out the bar herself. But going alone could be dangerous. Look at the trouble she'd gotten into at the more tourist-friendly vampire bar. If Rafe hadn't stepped in to stop that crazy guy from choking her...

Perhaps he could be persuaded to help her one more time. Was she crazy to ask a complete stranger for help? For all she knew Rafe Moreau could be involved in Julia's disappearance. Logic dictated she not trust him. But after the way he'd come to her aid, she couldn't bring herself to think he was the bad guy.

"Once Bitten, please," Claire instructed the cabbie as she climbed in. Relying on instinct was foreign to her. She usually made decisions only once she'd ascertained all the facts. But in these circumstances, her choices were limited.

When the cab pulled up to Once Bitten, there was a

line of people at the door waiting to get in that ended half a block away.

It was closed! She tried to see if there was an hours of operation sign. Peering between a guy with a huge mohawk and a fang-wearing Dracula look-alike complete with tuxedo and black cape, she saw a plaque by the door that read:

> *Open: Sunset*
> *Close: Sunrise*

Well, that was informative.

Maybe Rafe wasn't even working tonight. If he wasn't, how would she find him? And if he were, why on earth would he want to go with her to some place called The Pit after his shift was over?

This had been a stupid idea. Maybe she should just let the police handle it. What did she think she could do, anyway? What did she think Rafe could do?

Except… The look in his eyes when he'd threatened that crazy man… As if he'd seen things, had done things she wouldn't want to know about. There was something dangerous about Rafe Moreau.

If she could just get him to come with her. He'd dismissed her bribe the other night. But surely a large sum of cash could convince him. She hadn't seen a tip jar on the bar, and this crowd didn't seem like big tipper types. She'd have to have her dad wire her the money from her savings account. For Julia, she had to try.

Reluctantly Claire made her way to the end of the line. It was past sunset. Evidently the owner didn't keep a strict sense of time.

"Claire?"

She spun at her name spoken in that husky Southern drawl. "Rafe!" A burst of joy filled her chest. Then astonishment that she could feel such an emotion for a stranger. This situation was making her irrational.

"What are you doing here?" Rafe glanced around as if making sure no one he knew saw him speaking to her before his gaze settled solidly on her.

"I've come to make you a proposition."

His brows shot up.

"Not that kind of— It's not what you think, I mean, I wasn't—" God, she was stammering. Her cheeks were warm again.

His mouth slowly quirked up until he was smiling. Then he shook his head and chuckled. He took her arm and tugged her out of line. "Come on."

"Where are we going?" She allowed him to pull her along past the line of people waiting. He stopped at the front door.

"Inside." He dug into his jeans pocket, produced a set of keys and fitted one into the dead bolt of Once Bitten. He didn't stop the crowd from following them in, but he didn't head for the bar, either. Instead, he led her beyond the lounge area to another door, fitted a different key to its lock and ushered her through it.

"Take a seat." He dropped the keys on a sleek metal

computer desk and shrugged out of his worn black leather jacket, hanging it on a coat rack by the door. "Give me a few minutes, and then we'll talk." And he headed back out to the bar.

Claire blinked, taking in the room around her. The decor from the bar did not extend to this room. It was small, utilitarian. Obviously an office. One wall of exposed brick held a window covered with cheap beige blinds.

Dropping her purse, she sat in the black rolling chair and ran her hand over the desk. His scent lingered in the air. He must be more than a bartender for Once Bitten. This was his office.

Only, there were no knickknacks. No framed pictures of Rafe with friends or family. Nothing personal.

She considered herself a fairly private person when it came to her work environment, but even she had an electronic photo frame on her desk with a slideshow of herself with her family.

She did find a stack of business cards with his name, cell phone and website URL typed below Once Bitten. She took one and stuck it in her purse.

The door opened and Claire jumped up as if she'd been caught snooping.

"Okay, I have a few minutes." Rafe closed the door.

"You don't need to be tending bar?" Was she changing her mind about asking him?

"My assistant manager showed up. She's handling things for now. Tell me about this proposition." He leaned a hip against the desk as if this was just a casual conversation, but his eyes were fixed on her with an interested gleam. "Sit."

She sat back down slowly into the chair. While it had seemed a viable idea at the time, having to form actual words and say them out loud now seemed ludicrous. Perhaps she should leave it to the police.

Rafe folded his arms and raised his brows.

But while Sergeant Mulroney had said they would check out The Pit, the police were limited in their time and resources. They simply wouldn't have the manpower to stake out that bar night after night waiting for Shadow to show up. And moreover, a police presence there might actually scare Shadow away.

"Claire?"

Jerked from her thoughts, she looked up into Rafe's steel-gray eyes. "I want to hire you to— Well, as kind of a bodyguard, but more an advisor, you see, I don't want to go alone, but I need to know for myself if Julia is there."

"Hold on." Rafe put up a hand. "Where are you talking about?"

"It's a bar called The Pit." Suddenly she wanted to tell him about her day. "I did it, Rafe." She leaned forward, excited. "I found the lady that sold Julia's necklace. And she said the guy that sold it to her—with the blood drops tattoo?—his name is Shadow and—"

"No."

"No? No what?"

"I'm not going to The Pit. And you sure as hell aren't."

"If it's your time, I can compensate you. I'm willing to give you five hundred an hour. You're obviously the manager here, but if you need to call someone to work your shift…"

He'd begun shaking his head as soon as she mentioned the money.

"Seven-fifty an hour?" She was willing to pay whatever it took.

"Stop. It's not the money. I don't get involved in things like this. Call the cops."

"Oh, the police?" She narrowed her eyes at him. "Why didn't I think of that?" She grabbed her purse, stood and pushed her glasses up on her nose. Of course he didn't get involved. What had she expected?

But he had gotten involved last night.

She moved to brush past him and gave him her most withering glare. "And while I'm at it, I'll be sure to mention that *this* bar is the last place Julia was seen alive. I'll show them the picture in my phone she sent of her standing out in front of your sign outside." She reached for the doorknob.

"Hold on."

She turned to face him and almost stepped back at the fury in his narrowed eyes. "You're blackmailing me into helping you?"

She attempted a casual shrug of one shoulder, but the effect was ruined when her purse slipped and dropped to the crook of her arm. She raised her chin a notch. "I'll do whatever it takes to find my friend."

It took all her strength to remain composed while Rafe's scowl darkened and his hands curled into fists. Oh, no. She'd gone too far.

But then his expression cleared. He crossed his arms over his chest. "All right. Here's the deal. Tonight after my shift, I'll go check out The Pit. I'll watch for this Shadow guy and ask around. If I learn anything, I'll call you tomorrow, hell, I'll even call the police myself."

She couldn't believe it. She'd won. "That sounds great. Except I'm going with you."

"No."

"I'm perfectly capable—"

"No."

"But I can identify Shadow."

He let out a breath, half sigh, half growl. "Give me a description. You'd stand out like a vampire in a church."

"Oh." He was right.

He raised that infuriating brow again, as if to say, *obviously I'm right.* But she was far from defeated.

"What if I disguise myself? That way—"

"Look. That's my offer. Take it or leave it."

She frowned. Why didn't he want her there? She understood about standing out, but if she could blend in, she should be safe enough. Was there some information he wasn't disclosing? Was he even really going to go at all? Or just pop in and leave again? She sighed. How could she trust him when it could mean Julia's life?

But at this point arguing would be counterproductive. "Very well. I'll take it."

He narrowed his eyes, studied her a moment. Then he pointed his finger at her nose. "And if I see you there our deal is off, you got it?"

She scowled. "I got it."

4

WHY THE HELL HAD he agreed to do this?

Rafe sat in a back booth of The Pit nursing a double of bourbon and wincing at the punk rocker screaming his so-called song. And the stench of this place brought back memories of those early days on the streets.

It was a pungent blend of sweaty humans, spilt beer and piss. Not to mention the smell of burning pot and heroin. Yep, he'd once been right at home in a place like this.

His pappy had him drinking the hard stuff before he was thirteen, claiming he didn't like to drink alone.

If it hadn't been for ol' Earl…

This wasn't the time for reminiscing.

Rafe faced the front door, but so far no one fitting Shadow's description had come in. He'd looked in the back room around the pool tables already with no sign of the guy there, either. Shadow could've been in earlier, or he could not show up for days. This was a waste of time.

Having the police question him might've been slightly irritating, but Rafe could've handled it. The truth was he was here because she challenged him. *Dr. Claire Brooks.*

A PhD? She looked like the mad scientist kind. But her dumpy clothes and thick glasses hid an intelligent and fierce personality. He had to admire her loyalty to a friend. And the guts it took to brave a strange city and strange people. And to blackmail him.

He smiled to himself.

Rafe scanned the room again, thinking that, if not for sheer luck, he could've turned out like any of the scum in this joint. He stopped scanning and his gaze returned to a black-haired woman sitting at a table with two guys.

Her tight black dress plunged so low in front her large breasts spilled out to overflowing. Creamy, soft, plump breasts. His body tensed.

Damn.

He shifted in the cracked Naugahyde seat to get comfortable in his jeans. What the hell? He hadn't reacted this strongly to a set since he'd seen his first centerfold in a torn up *Playboy* he found in his pappy's closet.

And her legs. The dress barely covered her. Even wearing dark black hose and black biker boots her legs looked as if they went on for miles. Making her the perfect height to take her from behind. How easily he could picture holding her hips while he pumped into her.

Rafael Moreau, you dog. You're here to look for Shadow, not pick up a woman for the night.

One would think at thirty-four years of age he'd be past seeing women only as someone to get into his bed. But, he was what he was. At least he wasn't draping himself all over her and pawing at her like the two jerks sitting on either side of her.

She was obviously trying to keep their wandering hands at bay. But what did she expect in a place like this dressed like that?

Her raven hair was teased and spiked to stand up every which way. She wore heavy makeup, thick black liner and eye shadow, black lipstick. Her wide eyes were a soft doe-brown…

She glanced in his direction and quickly looked away.

Dammit.

He shot to his feet and stalked over to her table, gripped Claire's arm and hauled her to her feet. "What are you doing here?"

"Hey, man."

"Leave her alone, dude." The two men stood, taking up menacing stances. They stepped closer and Rafe could see their dilated, bloodshot eyes.

So he had called it right the first night he saw her. She was trouble. Well, he damn sure wasn't backing down from a couple of punks. He smiled at goon number one. "I'll give you one chance to leave peaceably."

Goon number one snickered. "What you gonna do,

old man?" He raised his fist, but before he could make contact Rafe punched him in the throat. The goon grabbed his neck and doubled over, choking.

"Rafe!" Claire tried to pull her arm free from his grasp, but he held on while he faced goon number two.

The second goon held up his hands palms out and backed away. "I'm good." He grabbed his still-choking pal and they scurried out the front door like the rats they were.

Rafe turned his scowl on Claire.

A split second of chagrin crossed her features before she raised her chin in that way that signaled she was bolstering her courage.

"I warned you if you came here the deal was off." He stalked back to the booth, grabbed his jacket and shoved his arms in the sleeves.

"Rafe." She stood in front him, blocking his exit. "I apologize, but I—"

"But, nothing." He sidestepped toward the door.

"I'd hoped that if I wore a disguise so I fit in, then I could also look for Shadow."

"Fit in? In that?"

She flinched.

He closed his eyes, gritted his teeth. He never raised his voice. But she'd been better off when she'd hid that body beneath the nerdy clothes. He cursed under his breath, turned and gulped down the rest of his bourbon, getting himself under control.

Those big brown eyes, just seconds ago full of defiance, were squinting. And she was biting her thumbnail.

Aw, hell. "Sit down." He resumed his seat.

She sat opposite him, her breasts jiggling as she scooted in.

He gritted his teeth and willed his gaze away from all that flesh. "Where are your glasses?"

"In my purse." She gestured to a small black bag slung from one shoulder across the other side of her body.

"Put them on."

She dug in her purse and slipped on the rectangular tortoise-shell frames.

He studied her, trying to find the frumpy woman from earlier today in the dark seductress sitting across from him. The thick lenses made her eyes look smaller. But they were the same soft brown. And the same directness stared back at him.

"No contacts?"

She shook her head. "Allergies." She sniffed as if just saying the word made her congested. He steeled himself against finding that cute.

"Those jerks could've had weapons."

"I know."

"I could've been killed."

She bristled. "I was doing fine until you came over and grabbed me."

"The hell you were!"

Her shoulders slumped. "You're right. I'm sorry."

Damn. She took the wind right out of his righteous sails.

"I don't blame you if you want to leave."

"You think I'm going to leave you here alone? You'll have the entire bar brawling within minutes. What's with that get-up, anyway?"

She looked down at her outfit, fingering the edge of her neckline. "I was trying to blend in. But I didn't try on the dress when I bought it. I usually just buy stuff and it fits..." Her voice trailed off as she looked back up and their gazes met. She bit her lip and her gaze skittered away.

When she returned her attention to him, her expression had taken on its usual haughtiness. "I appreciate your concern, and your help. And I'll pay you for your time. But I intend to stay here and watch for Shadow."

"Like hell you wi—"

She let out a soft gasp and her eyes widened. "Rafe! It's him!"

SHE'D FOUND HIM! Now Shadow was going to tell her what he'd done to Julia!

Claire scooted out of the booth keeping her eye on Shadow as he pushed through the crowd.

Rafe stepped in front of her. "Don't."

"Are you crazy? The only reason I'm here is to talk to him." She tried to step around him.

He grabbed her shoulders and glanced behind him.

Shadow was headed their way. "Confronting him won't help. I have a better idea."

Rafe yanked her glasses off and tucked her head into his shoulder, speaking low, "We'll follow him. See if he'll lead us to your friend." His breath tickled the sensitive skin beneath her ear and her cheek felt the rough stubble darkening his jaw.

Claire shivered in Rafe's arms. His masculine scent, his strength, his touch enveloped her, and something deep inside her responded.

Memories of how his stare had raked her body swamped her senses. He'd looked like a panther set to pounce on his prey. And she reveled in the attention. She'd never felt so desirable, so…sexual. This disguise released her from years of inhibitions.

When he lifted his head, their lips were millimeters apart.

To her horror, she moaned and his gaze dropped to her mouth. With a swift intake of breath he wrapped a hand around her nape, tilted her head back and took her mouth in a searching kiss. She whimpered and opened to him.

Her world became Rafe. His mouth moving over hers, his tongue exploring, possessing. The trail of heat left by his hands as they caressed her shoulder blades, her spine, her bottom.

With a growl he tightened his hold and everything in her wanted to take him inside herself. If she didn't stop him now, she'd give all to him right here in the middle of a bar.

She pushed him away, gasping for air. And sanity. This man was way more than she could handle.

Dropping his arms, he stepped away, his expression blank, seemingly unaffected. Except his lips were wet and his chest rose and fell slightly harder.

He scanned the place, presumably looking for Shadow. As she should be. How could she let herself be distracted by a carnal encounter when Julia was missing?

"He's in the back talking to some guy playing pool," Rafe said.

"My glasses, please?" She held out her hand.

He glanced at his hand as if he hadn't realized he held them, and then set them in her palm with a cocky smirk.

Rafe was right. Follow the creep. Hope that Julia was staying with him and that he'd lead them straight to her.

Retreating to the booth, she snuck a peek at Shadow. Rafe dropped into the seat across from her, signaled to the waitress and ordered drinks for them both.

Claire fidgeted, occasionally glancing into the back room. But she kept feeling Rafe's mouth on hers. Why had he kissed her? Was it just a ploy to prevent Shadow from recognizing him? But she thought he didn't know Shadow. *You're overanalyzing again, Claire.* It was just a kiss.

It was probably the stress of the moment. Her disguise had thrown him. She wasn't herself, and so he'd been more attracted to her Goth persona. How… depressing. She'd never been kissed like that. Rafe had kissed her as if his soul were on fire, with such smoldering passion that if it had gone on much longer she might have incinerated right there on the spot.

Her face was aflame just thinking about it. Avoiding his eyes, she dabbed at the perspiration at her temple.

Finally Shadow strutted over to the bar. He didn't look well. He was sweating heavily, his eyes darted around and his body twitched. Even she knew the signs of someone in need of a fix.

He appeared to be trying to wheedle the bartender into something, but he wasn't successful. When begging didn't work he pounded the bar. Whatever he yelled was drowned out by the deafening music. The bartender pulled a gun from somewhere and Shadow backed off. Then he shoved his way through the crowd of punkers and bikers and stormed out the front door.

Claire shot out of the booth with Rafe right behind her. He grabbed her hand and led her through the oblivious barflies.

Once outside, Claire breathed in the fresh air, while Rafe searched to the left, then the right. "There," he murmured and pulled her down the cracked sidewalk toward a darkened street.

She spotted Shadow, about thirty yards ahead of them, hurrying away on foot. Her heart pumped. She wanted to sprint after the guy and make him tell her everything he knew about Julia, but she walked beside Rafe at a normal pace.

When Shadow disappeared around a corner, Rafe sped up, pulling Claire along. His strong, callused grip gave her courage. She didn't feel so nervous.

At the corner, Rafe stopped and peered around the building before heading down the side street. Shadow was moving at a faster speed, and the dimly lit street made it more difficult to keep track of him. The farther they went, the less populated the area became. A lot of the buildings were boarded up or falling down and as they progressed, buildings gave way to empty fields. Ahead was an old graveyard, made eerie and sinister-looking by the fog.

She was getting nervous that they'd left civilization so far behind. Her feet hurt where the new boots rubbed, and she was freezing in the short dress. Shadow stopped at the graveyard, opened the creaky wrought-iron gate and entered.

Claire balked. The place was creepy. More rain threatened and she could barely see a thing. Panic hit her, an irrational fear caused by watching too many horror films.

"What is it?" Rafe whispered. He glanced at her but kept his eye on Shadow. "He's getting away."

She nodded, squeezed her eyes closed and then opened them. "Sorry." She took a deep breath and marched forward. Shadow was rounding a large crypt. Where on earth was he going?

Rafe opened the gate and hurried her through it before shutting it behind them. He darted from one large family vault to another until he came to the one Shadow had turned behind.

Nothing.

Shadow was nowhere in the distance. Nor anywhere they looked. It was as if he'd disappeared inside the tomb.

"Where'd he go?" she whispered.

"Hell if I know." Rafe dropped her hand and took off for the next large crypt.

"Wait!" No way was he leaving her alone in this scary place. She dashed after him, searching the area. No sign of Shadow. Once she caught up to Rafe, he strode off, this time openly searching around every large crypt and even trying to open the doors of a huge mausoleum that must hold dozens of family members.

The temperature had dropped. The fog had turned to an icy drizzle. She was shivering and her feet were in agony. Somehow Shadow had given them the slip. Hard to believe, but the guy must be smarter than he looked.

"Rafe." She touched his shoulder. "This is pointless. He's gone."

He looked at her and gave a curt nod. Then he stared out across the graveyard and cursed loudly. When he looked back at her, he scowled. "You're freezing. Why didn't you wear a coat?"

"I... It didn't go with my disguise."

"Unbelievable." He shrugged out of his leather jacket

and threw it around her shoulders. "Let's go. We have a long walk back."

Heat enveloped her. She slipped her arms through the sleeves and inhaled his heady scent. Part cologne and part the unique pheromones of the man, the fragrance made her insides ache and sent her libido into overdrive. Who knew she could be turned on just by a smell?

But Rafe had already stalked away and she rushed to catch up.

The walk back to The Pit seemed twice as long. Twice as dark and miserable. The boots she'd bought at the thrift store weren't quite her size. She'd have blisters tomorrow. Rafe no longer held her hand, but kept his hands tucked into his jeans pockets while marching a couple feet ahead of her, silent and morose.

She was grateful to make it back to his neighborhood. They may have been sinister-looking, derelict houses, but at least they blocked the cutting wind.

Her gratitude evaporated when a menacing figure materialized from between two buildings and shoved Rafe.

A scream stuck in her throat as he went down. The guy attacked Rafe, but Rafe kicked him, knocking him down. Rafe jumped him. In a blur, the two men fought, rolling on the ground. Claire heard the sound of punching fists and caught the glint of metal, and her heart leaped against her ribs.

Mentally kicking herself, she dug in her purse for her cell phone to call 911. Before she could get to it, one of the men called out in pain, then the attacker raced down the alley he'd come from.

Breathing heavily, Rafe gingerly got to his feet and then turned to her clutching a wicked-looking knife, the blade alone at least six inches long. There was blood on the back of his hand. "You okay?"

Shakily, she nodded, and he slid the knife into his boot.

Her whole body shook. She didn't know whether to be impressed or terrified. This man was much more than a bartender with a tough persona. How dangerous was he?

"Claire?" He took a step toward her, reaching out for her.

She instinctively stepped back.

He dropped his arm and his concerned expression hardened, devoid of emotion.

She blinked, realizing what she'd done. "I'm sorry, I—"

"We're almost back. In a few blocks you should be able to catch a cab." He gestured for her to precede him.

Guilt squeezed her chest as she walked past him. She felt his presence behind her, but the dynamics between them had changed. They were no longer allies. It was as if a brick wall had gone up between them. And it was her fault. He'd taken his personal time to check out The Pit for her. Chased a stranger halfway across town, and then defended her against an attack from who knows what kind of criminal, and she'd rewarded him with fear and suspicion.

She'd made such a mess of things.

And she was no closer to finding Julia.

Not for the first time in this debacle, tears stung her eyes. This whole situation seemed hopeless. What if she never found Julia? What if her best friend in the world became a cold case that never got solved? Or worse, what if she was already dead, her body lying in some ditch or thrown in the river?

As they came in sight of The Pit, Rafe pulled out a key from his pocket and headed for an old car that looked like it belonged in a junk yard. It was so late The Pit was closed, dark and quiet inside. And there were no cabs around.

Claire sniffed back her tears, struggling to contain them. Falling apart would not help Julia. She pulled out her phone to call the cab company.

"Just get in." Rafe stood beside his open driver's door, one arm resting on the roof, the other elbow propped on top of the door. "I'll drive you to your hotel."

With a final sniff, she hobbled to the car, opened the creaking passenger door and slid in. Rafe got behind the wheel and the loud engine roared to life.

She searched for a seat belt and finally found a lap belt and clicked it around her stomach. "Is this kind of seat belt even legal anymore?"

He shot her an incredulous look. "This is a nineteen-seventy-three Plymouth Barracuda. It's a classic."

"Okay. Sorry. I didn't realize." She glanced at Rafe as he steered away from the curb and made a U-turn on the street. His mouth was a grim line, and his jaw muscle ticked. She'd insulted him again.

She rode the rest of the way in silence and within a few minutes he'd pulled into the curved drive of the Les Chambres Royale and shifted into Neutral, staring straight ahead.

She cleared her throat. "Thank you f—"

"Forget it."

"I really apprecia—"

"You getting out?"

"I'm just trying to apologize for hurting your feelings."

"Heh," he snorted. "You didn't."

"Well, I would like to compensate you for your time. You—"

"Look, lady, just stay out of my life and we'll call it even, okay?"

An unreasonable ache lodged in her throat. She'd never been the touchy-feely kind. She must be especially tired. "Fine." She shoved her door open and jumped out, then remembered she still wore his jacket. She peeled it off, turned and tossed it onto the seat.

Trying not to limp, she'd barely reached the revolving glass door of the hotel when she heard his engine roar out of the drive. She stiffened her shoulders. With a hard shove she pushed her way into the lobby and strode to the elevators.

As the doors swooshed open, she stepped inside, pressed the button for her floor and then yanked off the wig. She didn't even want to think about how awful her hair looked. All she wanted was a long hot shower and to crawl into bed.

She would not think about why the thought of never seeing Rafe again made her stomach ache.

Julia should be her only concern.

As she stepped from the elevator onto her floor, she dug the antique key from her purse and made her way down the hallway to her room. Once inside, she hobbled into the bathroom, turned on the shower and then started stripping off the boots and hose carefully. She needed to get some Band-Aids for her blistered feet. She unzipped the dress as she limped to the bedroom, intent on throwing the black garment in the trash.

She froze, her heart pounding. All the drawers had been emptied, her clothes strewn about. She scanned the room. Her laptop was missing. Julia's suitcases had been dumped. The entire room had been ransacked!

Panicked, Claire raced for the door. The closet door opened in front of her and a familiar man jumped out with a laptop under his arm. It was Shadow! She froze and their gazes met. He saw that she recognized him. Before she could think what to do, he swung the laptop and bashed her temple. She hit the floor in blinding pain and dizziness. When she glanced up, Shadow had raced out of the room.

Shaking, and her head throbbing, she got to her

hands and knees and crawled to her purse. She grabbed her phone and Rafe's business card and dialed his cell.

He answered on the first ring. "Moreau."

At the sound of his soft, deep voice, a sob escaped. "Rafe! Shadow w-was here and he kn-nocked me down and stole my stuff and, and—" She stifled another sob. "P-please come?"

His phone clicked off.

5

RAFE STOMPED ON THE BRAKES and clutch before Claire had even finished her sentence. He downshifted and yanked the steering wheel sharply to the left, screeching the tires to make a U-turn. His only thought was getting his hands on that punk and beating him to a bloody pulp.

Crap. He'd hit the off button without telling Claire he was on his way. When he tried calling back her cell went straight to voice mail. Didn't matter. He'd be at the hotel in a few minutes.

When he pulled into the drive a police car was already there, lights flashing. He raced into the lobby. Damn. He didn't know what room Claire was in.

Two cops were standing at the elevator door. When it opened, he followed them inside. He could feel them scrutinize him, but he had as much right to be here as the next guy. He folded his arms and smiled at first one, then the other until the elevator door opened.

As he started following them to the room, they halted, hands on their gun belts and gave him the once over.

He smirked. Plenty of blow-hard cops had tried to intimidate him over the years. He lifted his chin. *Yeah, give it your best shot, buddy.*

They scowled, but turned and headed to the room.

A hotel security guard stood just inside the doorway. The police strode in and Rafe followed right behind them.

One of the officers blocked his way. "Sir, you can't come in here."

"The lady called me." Rafe shoved past the cop, heading for Claire.

The other cop seized him and wrenched his arm behind his back.

"Rafe!" Claire looked up, her eyes wide with fear. She ran to him as if he were some knight in shining armor. "You came."

His throat tightened. She was holding a bloody washcloth to her left temple. The woman had been through a lot. Her friend's disappearance, the knife fight and now a break-in. But he was nobody's damn hero.

The interrogating cop frowned at Claire. "Who is this?"

She blinked. "He's…a friend."

Rafe flexed his arm and snarled at the cop as he released him.

The other one pulled out a notepad and pen. "So, what happened here?"

As Claire told them about Shadow jumping out of the closet and knocking her down, her voice broke and Rafe fought the urge to tell the damn cops they'd have to interrogate her later.

"It sounds like an inside job," one cop said to the hotel security guy. "We'll need to question all the employees."

"Actually, I…might know what happened," Claire said quietly.

Rafe stilled.

"After I realized Julia wasn't going to meet me at the airport, I went to the police. But after that, I came back here and checked in again, requesting the same room in case Julia showed up and hadn't gotten my messages. And I…I left several messages letting her know I was in the same room."

The cop with the notepad frowned. "And you think this Shadow person is in possession of her phone and hotel key?"

Rafe gritted his teeth. Give the man a prize.

"Well, he had her necklace."

"That's the necklace the woman told you she bought at the flea market? And the lady at the flea market told you this Shadow person gave it to her to sell for him?" the same cop asked.

Claire nodded.

"Okay. We're already tracing your friend's cell number. Also, we'll need the make, model and serial number of your laptop. We'll start checking pawn shops."

Claire nodded. "Yes, of course."

"Anything else missing?" the other cop asked.

Claire looked around the room. "I don't think so."

"All right. We'll file a report and put out a BOLO for the perp."

"I need to tell you one more thing." She glanced at Rafe, as if asking for permission. He shrugged.

"Tonight, we saw Shadow at a bar called The Pit, and we followed him to a cemetery."

"The Saint Luis cemetery off Basin Street," Rafe provided.

Claire returned her attention to the cop. "But he disappeared. I guess he must've realized he was being followed and doubled back."

The cop gave her a disapproving look. "You need to let the police handle this from here."

"Yes, I know." She bit her lip as if she might break down and cry. But she drew in a breath and raised her chin. Something twisted in Rafe's gut when she raised watery eyes to the cop. "Sergeant Mulroney? Do you think there's a chance Julia is still alive?" Her voice faltered on the last word and her lips trembled.

"It's too early to say, Ms. Brooks. But we'll do everything we can to find her. In the meantime…" The cop raised his brows at the hotel security guard.

"Oh, yes." The guard cleared his throat. "Ms. Brooks, the manager asked me to offer his sincere apologies and assure you this won't happen again. We'd like to move you to the President's Suite."

"She's staying with me." Rafe blinked. Had he just said that out loud? First rule of the streets was take care of number one. He was losing his edge.

"I am?" Claire turned those big brown eyes on him. What had he just gotten himself into?

The police let Claire pack a few necessary items, but the room was a crime scene and more cops arrived to take pictures and dust for prints. They barely agreed to let her take a change of clothes.

An EMT showed up to check out her injury, closed up the cut with butterfly bandages and gave her some ibuprofen for the pain.

The cops took Rafe's name, address and phone number before allowing them to leave, and assured Claire they'd be in touch.

A strange sensation overtook Rafe as he drove her home. Half an hour ago he'd been glad to never see her again. Now, a part of him wanted to make her worries go away. Slumped in the seat of his Barracuda, she stared out the window biting her thumbnail, looking so lost and alone. He could relate to that.

It wasn't until he ushered her into his apartment above the bar that he thought about the sleeping arrangements. It was almost dawn. He was dog-tired.

Claire stood in the middle of his living-slash-dining-slash-bedroom, staring at the largest piece of furniture in his one room efficiency: his bed.

In this one thing, he'd indulged himself. It was a custom-made four-poster mahogany, with a pillow-top mattress and Egyptian thousand-thread-count sheets. He'd foolishly thought it might help his insomnia.

But sleep was overrated.

His new roommate had thrown on that disgusting crocheted poncho over the revealing black dress. She was right; it didn't go with her so-called disguise. Her hair had been flattened by the spiky wig and the black makeup she'd applied around her eyes had smeared.

How the hell could he find her attractive right now?

But his out of control mind kept seeing her naked in his bed, reliving the freakin' hot kiss they'd shared in the bar, and his body thought it was go time. The sleep-deprivation must be getting to him.

Not only was *Dr.* Claire Brooks injured and distraught, she was also not his type. Tourist girls were more his style. Young, pretty, looking for a fun fling and, most importantly, gone by the end of the week.

Although, Claire would more than likely be gone by the end of the week, too. The cops would probably find Shadow soon—if Rafe didn't find him first—and one way or the other, Claire would go back to Boston.

Forget it, Moreau. Remember, she's trouble in more ways than you want to even think about.

He strode to the tiny bathroom, flipped on the light. "Shower's here." He gestured to the mini-fridge. "I don't have much food, but there's some baguettes and coffee."

He waited a moment, to see if she had any questions, but she just stood there.

He shifted his weight to the other foot. "Get some sleep. I've got paperwork to finish." He headed for the inside stairway that led to the bar.

"Do you have to go?"

He froze. Her voice sounded so timid, so…needy. Flashes of their brief tongue tangle in The Pit stirred his libido. Her breasts pressed to his chest. His cock rose.

He turned back and met her gaze. "I need sleep and there's a couch downstairs."

"There's enough room in the bed for both of us to sleep."

His hands curled into fists. "*Cher,* if the both of us get in that bed we won't be sleeping."

Her eyes widened behind her glasses. She swallowed. "I know."

She sounded as if she was agreeing to be guillotined. He folded his arms across his chest. "Try to contain your excitement."

"I'm tired. And…nervous." She grabbed the hem of the poncho, lifted it over her head and tossed it on the floor. "I don't usually have one-night stands."

He narrowed his eyes. "Then why start now? Do I seem like a guy who needs your charity?"

She reached behind her and began unzipping the black dress, and at the same time toed off her short boots. "No. It's what I want." She closed the distance between them as she slipped her arms out of the sleeves and let the dress fall to the floor in a puddle around her feet.

Rafe's mouth went dry. Her only covering was a black lacy bra and matching boyshort panties. He looked his fill, from her long shapely legs, up her smooth creamy thighs, to her flat stomach, and especially the deep cleavage created by the bra. She wasn't petite, her hips were solid, and even in her bare feet she stood almost as tall as him.

As if she regretted undressing, her arms crisscrossed her body, uselessly trying to cover herself.

He gently moved them to her sides. "Maybe I do need this, after all." He lowered his head and pressed his lips to hers, nibbling and tasting. Lust had taken control at The Pit because he'd been blindsided by her transformation. Now, he wanted to take his time, savor her. Placing a hand at her jaw, he explored her mouth slowly with his tongue while his thumb caressed her cheek.

When she moaned and swayed into him, he smiled against her mouth. "Purr for me, *cher*." He tucked his thumb under her chin and angled her head back to allow his mouth access to her throat. Kissing down her neck, over to her shoulder, he slid one bra strap down out of the way of his lips.

He felt her skin quiver and her breathing grow shaky. His hand slid down and lowered her other strap, caressing her shoulders while his mouth moved down to the soft mound of her breast. Her sigh turned into a gasp as he nuzzled lower and licked her hard nipple over the rough lace.

He moved to her other nipple and then took it into his mouth to suck. She cried out and he smiled. She was so responsive. One arm under her butt, the other around her back, he half walked, half carried her the few feet to the bed and laid her down at the foot with her legs dangling off the edge.

She raised her arms over her head and stretched like a satisfied cat. He unbuttoned his shirt, yanked it off and tossed it. Behind her glasses, her eyes widened as she stared at his chest. Ah, his tat. But she said nothing.

Taking her hips in his hands, he dropped to one knee and kissed her stomach, letting his mouth travel down to the edge of her panties. Her breasts were still covered in black lace.

"Take off your bra," he rasped against her pelvic bone. Lifting his head, he watched as she reached behind her and unhooked her bra, and then drew it off slowly one strap at a time.

The bathroom light was thankfully bright enough to see the exact shade of her dusky-pink nipples. He could spend all night just caressing them, kissing them.

"You're beautiful." He had to taste one again. And he would. But first, to finish what he'd started. Curling his fingers under the edge of her lacy panties, he pulled the lacy fabric down to her knees, exposing pale pink flesh and dark curls. He groaned as he dragged the dainty underwear the rest of the way off her.

Beginning at her ankle, he stroked his hand up one leg to her inner thigh and spread her intimate folds.

When he brought his mouth to her soft sweet spot, she gasped and stiffened. As if she'd never had a man do that before. Geez, surely she wasn't… He looked up and caught her gaze. "This isn't your…first time, is it?"

She looked appalled. "No! Of course not!"

Thank God. He lowered himself and he whimpered and wiggled, encouraging him to continue.

And he was only just getting started.

6

CLAIRE COULDN'T BELIEVE she was lying here completely naked with some man's face.

Not just some man. Rafe. He used his fingers to open her more and then licked her and teased her until she couldn't hold in her moans. God, his tongue. His lips. She lifted her hips to him. The ache spiraled higher. She was so close to the edge, clasping his head with her hands and making incoherent noises.

It was exquisite. It was…embarrassing.

Stop that! Concentrate on how good it feels. How he teased her clit with just the right touch and speed. Oh, yes. It felt so good. Amazing. Getting closer. He must have done this to a multitude of women to know how to pleasure her so skillfully…. How many had lain where she lay now? And…it was gone.

What was wrong with her? Why couldn't she just relax and let it happen? She pushed him away and sat up, clamping her legs together and covering her breasts with her arms.

"What is it?" He huffed out a breath.

"I don't—" she squeezed her eyes closed and shook her head "—think I can do this."

He got to his feet, ran a hand over his mouth. "What are you talking about?"

"Oh, not sex, not you, I mean, you were great."

His scowl grew.

"It's me. I just can't…seem to…" She waved a hand. "Gregory said I'm too high-strung. I can't 'loosen up and let go.'" She used two fingers on each hand as air quotation marks.

With his hands on his hips, he stood there blinking, staring at her as if she'd just told him she was from another planet. She wished she could disperse into millions of molecules and *go* to another planet. "I'm sorry. I'll go."

She started to stand, but he caught her shoulders. "Hold on." He took her chin and tenderly turned her face to him. "Look at me, *cher.*"

She raised her gaze to his. His gray eyes were filled with determination.

"You're a beautiful woman."

Her instinct was to object, but his eyes bore into her, refusing to allow her to doubt his words.

His hand slid up to cup her breast, his fingers lightly touching her nipple.

She shuddered and felt both nipples tighten.

"Take off your glasses."

"But, I—"

He put a finger to her lips. "Shh. Do you trust me?"

Did she? It seemed kind of ridiculous to willingly expose herself to him this way if she didn't. But then again—

He chuckled. "You're thinking too much again, Claire. What does your gut say? Do you trust me? Yes or no?"

"Yes." She breathed the word.

He smiled and something inside her melted. Rafe brooding was sexy enough. But Rafe flashing a smile sent him into the handsome-as-sin category.

"Good." He brushed his knuckles across first one nipple, then the other.

She closed her eyes and arched into his hand. Before she opened her eyes again, he removed her glasses. "Keep your eyes closed," he said softly. He gently ran his fingers through her hair, brushing it away from her face until she felt her muscles relax.

"Scoot back and lie down." He lay on the bed beside her as she obeyed. He palmed her stomach, slowly stroking her skin. His hand glided up between her breasts then down to her stomach again, and then farther down, caressing her thighs.

He was being so patient. What if she couldn't— "Rafe?"

"Uh-uh-uh. No talking." He sighed. "Turn over." He

pushed her hip and she rolled to her stomach and rested her head on her folded arms.

"Keep your eyes closed." He began massaging her back, her shoulders. "Picture the mighty Mississippi, the water flows, lazily making its way down to the gulf."

She saw it.

"And there's a boat, just driftin' along." He gripped her behind one knee and bent her leg. At the same time he swept the hair off her nape and she felt his lips kissing there, and then down her spine. "The sun is warm." A soft kiss. "Birds are chirpin'." Another soft kiss. "You put your hand out and let your fingers dip into the cool water as you slowly drift down the river." Warm, sensuous kisses down the rest of her spine.

His breathy Cajun drawl lulled her into a languid state. She let out a sigh.

"Bon," he whispered. His hand traveled up from her knee to her thigh and slipped between them.

She moaned and raised her knee, giving him more access. His hand accepted the invitation and played with her, rubbing softly at first, then gradually using more pressure.

The pleasurable ache, the throbbing... Mmm, felt so good, and was building up to something more, and then more still. It felt as if she might burst, but she didn't want it to stop. She wanted even more, harder, faster, deeper, yes, deeper—and then an explosion of sensation unlike anything she'd ever felt before overtook her. She screamed, and her body tensed for what seemed like forever. She gasped for breath.

The throbbing eventually faded. Lazily she opened her eyes, taking in her surroundings. Remembering where she was.

She was on her back, with no memory of getting there. The muscles inside her still contracted like the aftershocks of an earthquake.

And that's what it had felt like. An earthquake inside her, erupting fiery lava, transforming her world. Transforming her.

And there was Rafe, a blurry shadow, but the white of his teeth flashed. "What does Gregory know, huh?"

Her face heated. "I just assumed it was me."

"Nothing wrong with you, *cher.*"

She smiled, cupped his face and rose up to kiss him. And kiss him and kiss him.

Squinting, she studied his muscled chest. A bold, black tattoo covered the top half of his right side. The abstract pattern started at the top of his right shoulder in a series of stark black swirls, or flames, each swirl ending on a fine point like a scythe. One of the scythes curved just under his right nipple. She wanted to lick that nipple.

With a hungry moan she stroked his pecs, and then slid her hands down to his stomach and back up, memorizing everywhere she touched. She licked her lips, pushed him to his back and leaned over him to place her mouth at his throat.

As she did, her breasts brushed his chest.

"I need these off." Her hands fumbled with his jeans.

He chuckled warm and long. "I've created a monster."

She grinned and palmed his erection through the denim.

"Hey!" He grabbed her trembling hand. "Careful now." He pushed to his feet and pulled a shiny packet from his wallet. Then he tugged his boots off, his jeans and boxer briefs followed and he lay beside her.

Even without her glasses, she could tell he was large and magnificently erect, the skin slightly darker than the rest of him. She wanted to touch him, to pleasure him the way he'd pleasured her.

She reached down and grasped him, feeling the soft skin covering a rod of steel. Her thumb rubbed the tip and spread moisture around the head. He groaned, pushing into her hand. "Won't take much more. I'd rather be in you, *cher*."

Moving a leg between hers, he rolled on top of her, resting his weight on his elbows. His penis pushed against her stomach. Deliberately, he took her right nipple into his mouth, drawing deeply and flicking his tongue across the peak.

"Rafe!" She cupped the back of his head and arched off the bed.

"I like that. Hearing you call out my name." He tore open the packet with his teeth, slipped on protection and then pressed into her to the hilt.

She wrapped her arms around his back, holding him tightly, running her fingers up into his hair.

"You feel good, *cher,* all tight and hot around me." His voice sounded strained, even muffled as it was against her neck. He started to move.

"You feel good, too." She arched her hips, matching his rhythm.

He groaned and pulled almost all the way out before thrusting back into her.

"Oooh, that feels good." She nuzzled into his neck. "Mmm, and you smell good, too."

He pulled out and pushed in again, powerful and hitting just the right spot. "Oh! Rafe? I should've told you at the hotel, thank you f—"

He stilled. "Claire?"

"Hmm?"

"No more talking now." He kissed her, long and deep as he moved inside her. His kisses trailed down her neck to her breasts where he suckled and his hands cupped, and played. She groaned and closed her eyes and pictured herself floating along the mighty Mississippi, its currents ebbing and flowing, gently tugging and pushing, and the pressure started to build again. Her hands caressed his back and shoulders. She was losing herself in the experience just like she had a few moments ago, and the aching, throbbing release was so close.

His rhythm sped up, and he slid a hand between them to rub and tease her and the next minute she was falling over the edge again. Rafe froze, then thrust once more, shuddering as he came.

Moments later, he moved next to her, his breathing erratic.

For a while there was nothing but colored lights behind her eyes and a thrumming in her veins. Gradually she began to notice the heat of the man beside her. Hear his breathing, feel the soreness between her legs and in her thigh muscles.

So this was passion. This was sex. This was the way it should be.

Sex with a man so purely male, so powerfully masculine he'd patiently brought her to, not one, but two miraculous orgasms.

She lifted up to study him, wishing she had her glasses on. He looked delicious, every broad-shouldered, big-muscled, long-limbed inch of him. Disheveled strands of hair fell across his eyes. She wanted to reach up and brush them away. But she didn't.

In this relaxed pose, he didn't look as formidable, but more like a little boy forced to become a tough man. Instead of looking peaceful, he looked tired. Lines of stress were more visible, and dark circles smudged his eyes.

What troubles weighed him down? She knew nothing about him except that he managed a bar, was good with a knife and was an exceptionally patient and determined lover.

How many other women had he brought here? Rafe had undoubtedly had dozens of one-night stands, maybe hundreds. Her nails dug into her palms at the thought.

Wait a minute.

Was she jealous? After having sex with him once?

"Why'd you call me?"

Claire jumped when he spoke. "What?"

He opened his eyes. "When I dropped you off at the hotel you thought I was no better than a thug with a knife. Why'd you call me instead of the police?"

"I did call the police."

He turned his head to look at her. "Fine." He sat up and rolled off the bed to his feet. "Hide behind semantics." Rafe disappeared into the bathroom.

"Wait." She frantically searched the bed for her glasses, squinting and feeling around with her hands until she found them.

As she slipped them on, he came back out, stepped into his underwear and jeans, tugged them up and zipped the fly.

Yanking the comforter up to her chin, she scooted to the edge of the bed, unable to meet his gaze. "I called you first because…because I knew you would make me feel safe. I was so scared, and I—I just…needed you there." She chewed her lip and waited for him to laugh.

Instead, he stepped close and touched his fingers to her cheek. "Tell me about you and your missing friend."

Claire blinked. "You want to talk about Julia?"

He shrugged. "Most people wouldn't go to these lengths for a friend, no matter how close they were." Striding to his makeshift kitchen—which was a small counter, a portable cooktop and a mini-fridge—he grabbed a can of grounds from the fridge and proceeded to make coffee.

"Are you coworkers?" While the coffeemaker gurgled and dripped, he retrieved his only chair from a tiny table by the window, turned it backward and straddled it.

"No. We go way back." She smiled, remembering when they were kids. How many scrapes had the two of them gotten into? Julia would suggest some outrageous stunt, Claire would dutifully list all the reasons why it was a bad idea and then Julia would coax Claire into doing it, anyway.

Her smile faded. "If you can believe it, I used to be even more of a geek than I am today. I'm sure you noticed my stutter."

"I did." Rafe got up and poured them each a mug of coffee. "Hope you like it black."

"Black is fine." She took the mug from him and sipped. "I was taller than most of the other kids, and shy, had the thick glasses." Wow, she sounded pathetic. She glanced at Rafe, but he looked interested, not disgusted.

"And Julia was gorgeous, blossomed early?" he guessed.

"Oh, no, she was a scrawny little thing." Always

hungry. And frequently dirty. Claire had eventually discovered that Julia's mother was an undiagnosed bipolar, incapable of caring for her own daughter. "Scrawny, but scrappy." She smiled. "She was fearless. One day this boy was bullying me during recess when Julia stepped in and bloodied his nose."

He whistled. "Julia punched some kid in the nose?"

"Yep." She nodded. "Got suspended from school for it, too."

His shoulders shook as he chuckled. "How old were you?"

"Third grade." Julia had become her best friend, her mentor, her sister.

"Gutsy kid."

"She was. After that we were inseparable until…" Until she'd left for Cambridge. Claire hadn't thought, until this moment, about how Julia must've felt when her best friend went off to an Ivy League university and left her in Missouri attending cosmetology school.

"Until?" Rafe urged.

Snapped back to the present, Claire answered, "Until I went to college. Which I might not have had the courage to do without Julia. I definitely wouldn't have gone to prom. But she had a way of making me believe in myself." She met Rafe's gaze with a determined glint. "And I owe it to her to believe in her now."

Rafe gulped his coffee. "But if she's such a daredevil, why are you so sure she hasn't just taken off on her own?"

"I'll admit, she sometimes does things on a whim without thinking it through. With Julia, taking risks was a lot of fun. But sometimes it got us into trouble. And Rafe, I know her. If she weren't in trouble, she'd be on the phone telling me all about her crazy adventure. We tell each other everything." She frowned into her coffee mug. "At least, we used to…."

Claire hadn't spent much time with Julia the past few years. Every time her childhood friend called to suggest a road trip, Claire had been too busy to go. Finally, last month, Julia had refused to take "too busy" for an answer.

It was their last year to be twenty-something, Julia had cajoled. She'd promised Claire would only miss two days of work, tops. So, despite being in the middle of a huge project at the lab, Claire had agreed to meet Julia in New Orleans for Mardi Gras.

And look where it had gotten them.

Could Julia be punishing her for the past years of neglect?

Rafe was still watching her intently.

"Did you know an average of three hundred and fifty thousand women are reported missing every year?"

"Uh—"

"That's nine hundred and fifty-eight a day! Two hundred and thirty-three thousand women in the U.S. are raped or sexually assaulted."

"You just happen to have all these statistics in your head?"

"I looked them up while I was sitting in the police station the first day."

"And you remembered them?"

She shrugged. "I have a good memory for numbers."

He just blinked.

"And also, government research shows that victims of nonfamily abductions and stereotypical kidnappings are most at risk of injury, sexual assault or death."

Rafe frowned, examining his mug. "That doesn't mean—"

"I know." Dwelling on what-ifs wouldn't do Julia any good. Claire took a sip of her coffee. "This is good coffee," she said to change the subject.

He grunted. "You want more?" He swung a leg behind the chair and went to the coffeepot.

"No, thanks. I'd never get to sleep." The sun was gradually lighting the room. Traffic noise was revving up for the day. She could faintly hear the bells of the St. Luis Cathedral ringing in the distance. Claire yawned and her eyelids were heavy, but she didn't want their conversation to end.

She watched him refill his mug. He performed even this simple chore as deftly and masterfully as he did everything else. "You don't just manage Once Bitten, do you? You're the owner."

Returning to his chair, he raised a brow. "How'd you guess?"

"You don't seem like the type to take orders well."

Rafe couldn't help a chuckle. Claire was astute, he'd give her that. And not just that. She'd surprised him several times with her courage, and her stubbornness, and her loyalty to a friend who probably didn't deserve it.

And all that passion kept tamped down, like a banked fire just waiting for someone to come along and stoke it up into roaring flames. And she'd set him ablaze, as well. She'd been so tight. So hot. He'd lost himself for a moment.

Was that why he'd been attracted to her? He'd sensed something inside her, a tension, a cord wound tight, ready to snap.

"So, how did you come to own a vampire bar?" As if she was readying herself for a long bedtime story, she scooted back, lay down and pulled a soft fluffy pillow under her head.

A woman. In his bed. He'd never brought a woman up here. It was much easier to go to their place—usually a hotel room—so he could leave whenever he wanted. And never have to talk afterward.

Damn, he shouldn't have asked about her life. Now she thought she could question him. He could tell her he needed to finish that paperwork downstairs. But... "I grew up in New Orleans."

He found himself standing, making his way to the

bed and leaning against the bedpost. "My first job was in a bar. O'Sullivan's down on Picayune. Cleaning up, doing whatever." He didn't tell her he'd learned to make most drinks before he was fifteen. "Didn't take me long to realize somebody like me's not going to get anywhere working for other people."

Her gaze seemed to penetrate his protective shield. "People like you?"

He gritted his teeth. She could stare with those big brown eyes all day. He sure as hell wasn't going to spill his guts to this woman. "Let's just say I'm no doctor."

"I'm really just a microbiologist."

"Oh, well. That's different, then."

Her lips flattened. "So, why a vampire bar?"

He shrugged and finished his coffee. "It's a way to stand out. Tourists love it." Despite the coffee, his body was screaming for rest. His mind must need sleep, also, or he would never have talked so much about himself. And Claire looked damned sexy lying there all curled up in his satin comforter. He pushed off the bedpost, crawled in beside her, gently removed her glasses and set them on the bedside table.

Claire rolled to face him, reached over and ran her palm down his chest. Her hand felt soft and warm, soothing…

That was the last thing he remembered until he woke from another nightmare about his pappy. The old man was yelling at him again, had the belt out, threatening like always to beat the crap out of him. But this time Pappy was raving about what a sad sack he was for letting Shadow get away.

And Rafe woke up knowing he was right.

7

CLAIRE WOKE FROM A profound sleep, smiled and stretched in the big soft bed with the silky sheets. She hadn't slept this well since—

Julia! The events of the past three days came slamming back, jolting her fully awake. She twisted and saw the empty space beside her.

Rafe was gone.

From the amount and angle of the light coming through the blinds, it was probably late afternoon. She listened, but heard no shower running. No music blaring from downstairs. Perhaps he was just finishing that paperwork he'd mentioned.

She had things she needed to take care of also. She wanted to call Sergeant Mulroney and see if they'd had any leads on Shadow or the laptop. If Shadow pawned it, hopefully there'd be surveillance tape from the store.

She found her purse, grabbed her cell and called, but the sergeant wasn't at his desk. As it was Sunday, checking in with her office would have to wait until tomorrow. And she put off calling her parents, knowing she needed to share what information she had, but… she wanted a little while longer to bask in this blissfully sated feeling.

As she stepped into the shower, she contemplated the astounding events of this morning. Aside from the fact that she'd never experienced orgasm before, she'd never—not ever, been told she was beautiful—parents didn't count. Not in this way. Not in the way Rafe had said it. As if he meant it. As if he actually saw her as a person of beauty. And she'd certainly never felt such white-hot desire. She'd assumed it just wasn't in her. She'd been blessed with a high I.Q. and that—she'd believed—meant sacrificing other things. Like passion.

Half an hour later, feeling refreshed and in a clean change of clothes, she cautiously made her way downstairs. Her stomach was growling. Perhaps she could talk Rafe into going to the Café Du Monde with her and they could order beignets and café au lait.

At the bottom of the stairs, the spikey-haired, shaved head lady stepped into her path. She glared at Claire, then her gaze darted past her, up the stairs and back to her again. Her eyes narrowed. "I see the King of Flings has bagged himself another Mardi Gras conquest."

Claire flinched, feeling suddenly self-conscious having been caught coming from some guy's apartment. A virtual stranger.

"Aw, did he make you think you were special?" She

pretended to pout. "Don't worry, honey. That's his forte." She curled her lips and stalked out the back door to the parking lot.

Claire's face was blazing hot and the room seemed to spin for a moment. The venom from that woman was enough to fell an elephant. But the heavy dose of reality was exactly what she needed right now. Had she actually started to go all moonbeams and starlight about this guy?

As she entered the bar, she steeled herself to face Rafe by thinking about her next plan of action to find Julia. Except she had none.

The bar was dark and empty, somehow seeming even more eerie and frightening for its lack of patrons. She pictured pasty-white beings asleep inside the coffins waiting for the sun to go all the way down before throwing off the lids and rising to feed upon unsuspecting tourists.

With a shiver she turned to the office, assuming she'd find Rafe.

As she opened the door, Rafe spun lightning fast to face her, aiming a large, black handgun. At her.

Her heart seized up. Her throat closed. She couldn't breathe.

"Damn it!" He glared at her before pointing the weapon at the ceiling. "Don't ever come in here without knocking." There was a deadly edge to his voice, and his eyes were a hard, slate-gray.

"I'm s-sorry."

Still glaring, he clicked something on the gun and a clip slipped out. And, just like in cop shows, he checked the chamber, then shoved the magazine back in again. But he looked nothing like a cop. Dressed in a tight gray T-shirt and low-riding jeans, he looked like a thief who'd come to rob this place instead of its owner.

He stood and gently laid the gun on his desk. "Did you need something?" Without looking at her, he grabbed a small box from his desk drawer. The assistant manager was right. Obviously she was nothing special to this guy. Why would she be?

"I—I thought I'd get something to eat."

He glanced at her, pulled an extra magazine from the box and shoved it into his back pocket. "I have to work."

"And you need a gun to work?"

He hesitated a millisecond too long. "Everyone in this neighborhood keeps a gun behind the bar."

"I see." But she didn't. She also didn't believe him. What was he planning to do with it? Was she totally naive to trust this guy? Her stomach heaved.

Maybe he was going back to The Pit. But why would he, when the police could handle it from here forward? He'd made it clear from the beginning he didn't want to get involved. And why not tell her, if that was his plan?

Because he didn't want her tagging along, getting in the way.

But still, something wasn't right.

For once, Claire, go with your gut, Julia would have said. But Claire didn't place much faith in *her* gut.

"Something else you need?"

The way he asked made her wince. As if she were bothering him and he couldn't wait for her to get out of his sight. As if they hadn't been as intimate as two people can be not eight hours ago.

But what did she expect? An undying declaration of love just because they'd had sex? She knew better.

But it still…hurt.

"No, nothing."

She went back upstairs, grabbed her purse and called a cab. But instead of asking the driver to take her to the police station, she had him park out of sight of the bar, but with a clear view of where Rafe's Barracuda would emerge from.

Rafe had taught her one useful thing.

Don't confront.

Follow.

LESS THAN TEN MINUTES LATER, Rafe's Barracuda appeared at the corner of Dauphine Street and turned right onto Bienville.

Claire's cab followed, but kept a safe distance as Rafe drove farther away from the French Quarter. Up onto the freeway headed toward Lake Pontchartrain, he was driving into a less affluent suburb of New Orleans. There were a couple businesses that had been boarded up, a vacant shopping center surrounded by overgrown weeds. And small, ramshackle houses that had seen better days. This was the kind of poverty-ridden area that bred hopelessness.

How did he know to come to this area? Her chest hurt to think he might be meeting Shadow here, conspiring with him. She just couldn't believe that of Rafe.

The Barracuda made a U-turn, disappearing under a bridge about a quarter of a mile ahead. The overpass was one of several freeways all crisscrossing each other, forming six to eight clover-shaped viaducts overhead. None of which had any lighting beneath them.

She ordered the cab to pull into a twenty-four-hour convenience store parking lot a few blocks before the overpass, and then twisted in her seat to watch for Rafe's car to appear on any of the highways. But no black Barracudas came into sight.

Spinning back around, she huffed out an irritable sigh. The other side of this bridge was a dead-end unless one U-turned back onto the freeway. If he'd somehow realized she was following, he might be sitting over there, idling, possibly waiting for her, or maybe he hadn't, and had parked and was on foot.

She could either have the cab take the U-turn and risk Rafe seeing her, or wait here and possibly miss whatever Rafe was doing. Or she could sneak over there on foot.

Digging into her purse, she found her pepper spray, paid the cabbie and asked him to keep the meter running and wait, then swung open the door and gingerly stepped out.

Her stomach cramped and her whole body tensed

as she all but ran down the sidewalk, casting quick glances at the people around her. Most just stared, but two young men started following her, their shaved heads and thick chains looped from their jeans gleamed in the freeway lights above.

She drew a ragged breath and prepared herself to cross the street away from the well-lighted store and into the murky shadows under the bridge where the Barracuda had disappeared.

Glancing behind her at the two skinheads following her, she put her finger on the button that activated her pepper spray and picked up her pace. The footsteps behind her sped up, as well. Her heart pounding, she made it to the other side of the underpass to find herself in a deserted field where several junked cars had been abandoned. And one black Barracuda parked by itself.

The delinquents behind her caught up and she spun, raising her can of pepper spray. But she fumbled the button and dropped it.

Both guys covered their eyes until they noticed nothing had happened. Then they grinned.

She turned and ran, scanning the area for any sign of Rafe.

"You don't trust me, Claire?"

She yelped as Rafe stepped out from behind a huge cement support column for the highway overhead, his arms crossed in front of him.

"Rafe!" She flew into his arms, shaking in terror. Her heart couldn't take much more of this.

For a moment his arms came around her, held her tight. Then he grabbed her shoulders, shoved her to his side and reached behind him, producing the gun. He aimed it at the two thugs, who were only a couple of feet away. "Beat it!"

The two backed off, cursing and using crude hand gestures.

After they were gone, he dropped his arm and turned to her. His lips—the same lips that had so sensuously pleasured her in the wee hours of this morning were a tight, hard line. And his eyes practically spit fury. "I ought to leave you out here to the mercies of those two."

Claire blinked, looked back at where the skinheads had been and then returned her gaze to Rafe and swallowed. "I—I was only following your advice."

His eyes flared, a spark of surprise in them.

Rafe spun on his heel and strode away, tucking the gun into the waistband of his jeans at the small of his back. He headed farther into the cluster of highway overpasses, where the bridges came closer together and formed a huge covered area.

Claire hurried to catch up and glimpsed light flickering ahead. As she got closer, she saw it was a fire burning in a metal trash can, with a small group of people huddled around it for warmth. How cold they must get, exposed to the elements 24/7.

She stilled.

As she looked around, she saw dozens more, men, women and children sitting around, in makeshift beds of newspaper and cardboard boxes, or tattered bedrolls. Some even had tents pitched on the concrete.

A lump formed in her throat, and her heart squeezed. They were the nameless, faceless victims of mental illness or just plain poverty. The homeless.

Rafe had marched on ahead and stopped at a circle of rough-looking men. One by one, he clasped their hands and thumped their backs as if they were old school chums. They stood around talking, some shaking their heads, others nodding.

Why had Rafe come here? Several scenarios raced through Claire's mind. Did he think Julia had gotten high and was wandering around lost? Not a bad theory, except the Julia she knew didn't do any drugs. Was it possible she didn't know Julia as well as she thought? Claire had to squeeze her eyes shut at that notion.

An old woman, her hair straggly, her face reddened from the cold, approached her, wheeling a rusted metal shopping cart. "You a friend of Rafe's?" Her voice was scratchy, her teeth brown or missing.

A friend? Claire decided that accurately describing their relationship didn't matter. What mattered was information. "Yes. He's helping me look for a friend of mine who's missing. Her name is Julia." She grabbed her cell from her purse, pulled up Julia's picture and showed it to the lady. "This is her. Maybe you've seen her?"

The lady looked at the picture and shook her head. "Rafael's helping you?" She looked disbelieving, and then narrowed her eyes as she perused Claire from head to toe and back up again. "Why?"

"Excuse me?"

"Why's he helping you?"

"Uh, I suppose because my friend was last seen in his bar."

Her face scrunched up in a threatening snarl. "You tell the cops that? You get Rafael in trouble with the cops?"

"No! I—" Was that the only reason he was helping her? That thought left a bad taste in her mouth. She must be sure to tell him she wasn't going to hold that over his head. "Do you know a guy who goes by the name of Shadow? He's tall and thin, with dark hair, and he has three blood drops tattooed down the left corner of his mouth."

The woman shook her head and kept shaking it. Then she poked Claire hard in the chest. "You hurt our Rafael and you'll be sorry." Her voice rose. "I'll get the voodoo on you!" She started screaming incoherently, shoving Claire. Claire tried to reassure the woman, but it didn't help.

Rafe appeared, put his arm around the old woman. "'S'all right, Ima Jean, everything's all right now." He spoke in that soft Cajun accent and rubbed her arm and soothed her hair back from her brow.

For Claire he had nothing but a cold glare before he turned the woman back toward the group by the fire. Once he had her settled, he stalked over to Claire.

"Let's go." He took her arm and started dragging her away.

And she let him. Whatever he'd come here for, he'd done it. And he wasn't going to tell her what it was unless he wanted to.

But it all made sense now. The air of danger about him. The skill in knife fighting. The familiarity with a gun. She'd discovered a missing piece of the puzzle that was Rafe—Rafael Moreau. A piece, she guessed, most people didn't know. A piece that made her want to know even more about him.

Rafe had once lived on the streets with these people.

RAFE PULLED CLAIRE along to his Barracuda, barely keeping himself in check. He was tired. So tired. And pissed. And he had no patience for Ms. Stick-Her-Nose-in-His-Business. Although, strictly speaking, this was her business. But she just needed to let him handle it, damn it.

He'd felt like a full-on hero when she flung herself into his arms earlier. Her breasts had pressed against his chest and he'd wanted to lower his nose to her neck and breathe in her clean scent.

But he'd been forced to pull his Sig Sauer like the banger he used to be.

How the hell else was he supposed to keep her safe when she came into this part of town looking like she did? Wait. Since when had he found jeans and a Harvard sweatshirt sexy? But something about the dark red color of the shirt brought out red lights in her brunette hair, which curled delectably out of control as usual. He wanted to reach up and twirl a short silky strand around his finger

He shook his head. He was losing it.

"Wait." She dug in her heels when he tried to push her into his passenger seat. "I've got a cab waiting on the other side of the highway."

Merde. "Get in." He started the engine, swung around and paid off the cabbie before roaring back onto the highway. Maybe it was the adrenaline from the danger, but all he wanted to do was toss her in the backseat, pull up her shirt, drag off her jeans and be inside her again.

"You were seeing if any of your friends knew Shadow? Or where we might find him?" Claire asked.

Rafe forced his thoughts to the problem at hand. "Yeah. I called in some favors. They'll put the word out. If anyone knows anything, they'll come to the bar."

She nodded. "Thank you."

He shrugged, irritated. With himself. With her. With the whole foolish situation. He shifted gears. Changed lanes.

"I'm sorry I upset Ima Jean."

Rafe glanced at Claire as he punched the clutch and shifted a second time. She was biting her thumbnail and he wanted to take her hand and suck that thumb into his mouth. "She doesn't like outsiders."

Claire gently cleared her throat. "After the last housing bubble burst, I believe the number of homeless rose to around seven-hundred thousand. Ten percent of U.S. workers' incomes decreased to below the poverty level, and especially in New Orleans after Katrina—"

"What would you know about it?" He gritted his teeth at her arrogance. "Spouting your facts and figures? Have you ever had to wonder where you were going to sleep at night? Ever gone even one day without food?"

"You're right. I can't even imagine what that must be like." She moved in her seat to face him. "Were you displaced after Katrina?"

He scoffed. "I was in the Gulf on a rig when Katrina hit. What happened here after the hurricane only confirmed what I already knew. You can't count on anyone but yourself."

He glanced over at her. She frowned as if she were trying to figure him out. "Were your parents…drowned in the flood?"

Clenching his teeth, Rafe changed lanes to pass an eighteen-wheeler. "My parents died when I was twelve."

Her mouth dropped open. "I'm so sorry."

He shrugged. "It was a long time ago." Then why did he still feel like slamming his fist through a wall?

"What happened?"

They were almost to Once Bitten. The wheels screeched as he turned into the alley behind his bar. His lungs felt tight as he parked and killed the engine. "Head-on collision."

"Oh, my God." She reached out a hand to touch his shoulder, but he opened his door and jumped out.

"I've got to open the bar." He slammed his door, and then took the stairs two at a time to get to his apartment.

His keys. He'd left them in the damn car. He turned and Claire was behind him. Holding his keys.

"Rafe."

"Give me the keys."

"Are you okay?"

"Give me the damn keys!" He snatched them from her fingers and unlocked the door. Slamming open the door, he made a dash for the cabinet under the sink and grabbed the bottle of whiskey. By the time he had the lid unscrewed and the bottle to his mouth, she was standing next to him. He avoided her gaze and took a swig. And then another, longer gulp.

"Rafe."

"Dammit!" He slammed the bottle on the counter, ready to tell her to mind her own stupid business.

Someone pounded on the door leading to the bar. "Rafe, you there?" his assistant manager, Rowena, yelled.

Rafe blinked, pulled out his cell and checked the time. Damn, Ro had already opened the bar. What the hell was he doing? He squeezed the bridge of his nose and strode to the door. "I'll be right there," he called. He didn't know what had happened just now, but, thankfully, he didn't want or have time to think about it.

"Got a message for you, Rafe." Rowena spoke through the door.

Claire pulled a tissue from her purse and wiped her nose.

He opened the door. "What is it, Ro?"

"There's a guy here says he has some information for you about someone named Shadow."

8

"Put him in my office. I'll be right there," Rafe calmly told Ro.

Ro nodded and headed back down the stairs, but not before giving Claire the evil eye.

Rafe closed the door and swept past Claire.

He jerked out of his jacket, strode to the bathroom and splashed water on his face.

Claire followed, standing in the doorway. Her gaze caught the handle of the gun sticking out of his waistband.

Rafe straightened, wiping his face with a towel. He caught her gaze in the mirror. "What?"

"I just wanted…" What could she say? *I want to know everything about you, Rafael Moreau. What happened to you after your parents died? Why can't you talk about it?*

"You want to find your friend or don't you?" He

gestured toward the stairs, and Claire preceded him down to the bar.

At the door to his office, she waited for him to enter first before following.

"Rafe." An older man who looked to be in his forties fist-bumped Rafe. He was easily half a foot taller than Rafe, with a thick neck and a broad chest. His salt-and-pepper hair was tied in a ponytail at the back of his neck and the tail was a couple of feet long. But his straggly beard was completely gray.

"Hawk, how you doin', *mon ami*." He offered the man the chair, but Hawk shook his head, folded his beefy arms and stared pointedly at her.

Claire shrunk into herself, then harnessed her inner Julia, lifted her chin and returned his stare.

"She's with me." Rafe gestured at her, and Hawk's eyes widened, and his gaze moved down her body, and back up again.

"Heard you're looking for a low-life called Shadow."

"You know him?"

"Yeah. He's small time, steals enough to get high."

"Know where I can find him?"

"I know where he used to be, man. But I heard he was recently…excommunicated, let's call it."

Rafe folded his arms and leaned against his desk. "It's a start."

"There's this group of people that believe they are vampires, call themselves The Colony. They don't break the law, but they don't exactly like it when members try to leave, if you know what I mean."

Rafe nodded. "I've heard of them. A few used to hang out in the back room here sometimes. They're a cult of sorts. Rumor has it they like to drink each others' blood as a turn-on. But from what I saw they were basically harmless. Know where I might find them?"

A cult? Claire shivered. They didn't like it when members left? Could Shadow have brought Julia there and now they were holding her against her will? And what was that part about drinking each others' blood?

"Okay, thanks, man." Rafe straightened from the desk and briefly clamped Hawk's upper arm. "I owe you."

She'd missed Hawk's answer. About where to find them. As Hawk approached the door, Claire stepped aside, but extended her right hand. "Thank you."

His huge hand swallowed hers. Rough calluses scratched her palm, but he smiled as he looked down at her. "If you're Rafe's woman, no need for thanks." He opened the door and was gone before she could correct him.

Rafe's woman. She had to admit that the sound of that sent a thrill through her.

Get real, Claire Brooks. You're nothing but a pain in Rafe Moreau's behind. An annoying fly he'd like to swat. At best, you were a fling.

"So." Rafe pulled the gun from his waistband and set it on the desk, took a seat in his chair and gathered up some papers. "Now you can tell the cops to check out The Colony." He began scrutinizing the papers as if the secret to immortality were hidden in them.

Dismissed. As if he were one of her professors at the university and she were one of his students. Class over. *We're over.* Except, despite Hawk's assumption, they'd never been a *"we."*

Oh, but she would never forget his lovemaking. The memory would keep her toasty warm on many a bitterly cold Boston night to come.

Rafe cleared his throat. "This paperwork isn't going to finish itself." He raised a brow at her, then returned his glare to the ledger on his desk. Did he remember why he hadn't gotten to it earlier?

"Right." She pulled out her phone, brought up the sergeant's number from her list of outgoing calls. "I'm sorry, what was the address? I didn't catch it."

"It's the old abandoned hospital in New Awlins East," he mumbled, still engrossed in the ledger.

"East. Right. What was the name of the hospital?"

He jerked his gaze to her, narrowing his eyes. "Don't even think about it."

"What?" She was a terrible actress. Still, she gave him her most innocent look.

"I mean it. You go out there tonight and I'll shoot you myself."

"Rafe, what if she's being held prisoner there?"

"Let. The cops. Handle this."

She let out a defeated breath and punched Mulroney's number.

The phone barely rang before the sergeant answered. "Mulroney."

Rafe snatched the phone from her hand and proceeded to fill in Mulroney on everything they'd learned from Hawk. Then he warned the sergeant that Claire might try to head there herself and they should send someone now. She couldn't hear what Mulroney said next, but Rafe swore under his breath, clicked the phone off and leveled a cold stare at Claire.

"Let's go." He grabbed his gun, stuck it back in his waistband and strode out of his office.

Confused, Claire followed.

"Ro, I'm going out," he called to the woman behind the bar serving customers. Then he raced up the stairs to his apartment.

Claire hurried after him. "What did Mulroney say? Aren't they going to check it out?"

"As soon as they can spare a patrol car." Rafe grabbed his jacket and his keys and headed out the back door.

"I don't understand. After the break-in at the hotel, he seemed to take Julia's disappearance more seriously." She rushed down the stairs after him.

Rafe gave a humorless laugh. "He said if she *is* with this cult, then it's of her own free will."

"No! Julia would never do that."

"That's what cults do, Claire. Brainwash suckers into believing in their craziness."

She hesitated. Could she again let him put himself in possible danger for her? This group, this...Colony, were really just regular people, after all. But they might not appreciate Rafe and her barging into their midst and trying to extricate Julia. And they drank human blood?

But what if Julia was being abused even as Claire stood here dithering?

Images flashed before her of Julia's wrist being cut and her wound forced to bleed into a chalice, or even her neck being bitten, or of her sexually assaulted by some delusional sadist.

Claire bit her lip, constricting her distress. "Rafe?"

"What?" He half turned back.

"If Julia *is* there, but it seems too dangerous to confront them, we call Sergeant Mulroney and wait for him to bring backup. Deal?"

He raised his brows. "Who said anything about confronting them?" He continued down the stairs.

BY THE TIME RAFE PULLED the Barracuda into the cracked, weed-infested parking lot of what used to be the Delacroix Asylum on the outskirts of Orleans Parish, he was wondering if he should have his head examined. What was he thinking coming out here to rescue some bimbo who probably didn't want to be saved?

Hell, they weren't even sure she was here.

Then he grinned at the irony of using the phrase *head examined* at a place like this. More than likely the poor souls who'd ended up here had had their heads cut open for a lobotomy.

He shuddered, but covered it by getting out, striding to the back of the Barracuda and opening the trunk. He pulled out his two-foot-long Mag-light. The sucker weighed a good five pounds and, if wielded properly, could cause a concussion.

"Here." He handed it to Claire.

She turned it on and aimed it at the crumbling building.

"If you need it, that thing makes a pretty good weapon."

Her eyes wide, she looked back at him and then down at the flashlight. "Okay."

He took her elbow and guided her toward the entrance.

Claire was studying the building. "This used to be a hospital? It looks more like an old plantation house." They took the dozen steps carefully, avoiding rotted-out planks.

"It was. Then, during the Civil war, it was used as a hospital. By the early twentieth century, it'd been turned into an asylum."

She glanced at him. "How do you know so much about it?"

"The Delacroix Asylum used to be a stop on all the ghost tours until the building was officially condemned."

She rubbed her arms and shivered. "Condemned?"

He chuckled. "That's what bothers you? Not the ghosts?"

"I don't believe in ghosts. Do you?"

"*Cher,* I'm from New Awlins. I was raised on all kinds of supernatural stories from ghosts and ghoulies to voodoo and vampires."

"Well, I'm from Missouri. The 'Show Me' state."

He caught her mouth curving up at the corners. A beautiful mouth, full lips. He wanted to taste them again. Wanted to feel them on his skin again. And… yeah, he must need his head examined if he could think of sex right now. An hour ago he would've sworn he wanted nothing more to do with Claire and her mission. He'd done all he could and the police would handle it from there. He didn't want to get any more involved.

But then she'd looked at him with those big brown eyes, damn it. Maybe he *could* use a lobotomy.

"Is it safe to go inside?"

The porch had a hole about five feet in diameter where the worn wood had broken. He shrugged. "If we're careful." Gingerly, he stepped around it and opened the double doors, noting the chain was missing that should be locked around the handles. A good sign that someone was using the place. Or had been recently.

It struck him that he and Claire were behaving like the morons in those horror films who go into the spooky mansion even after all their friends have already been slaughtered by the psychotic murderer. But he squelched the thought—after all, there'd been no murders committed. And he'd met a few of the members of this cult before. They weren't violent.

Claire lighted the way, but he went in first. She stepped inside behind him and shone the beam of light all around. The twenty-foot-tall arched ceiling was impressive, until a closer look revealed the once-gilded wood was rotting. What was left of the blue silk wallpaper was peeling. And the floor was more moss and weeds than pine planks.

"There are an awful lot of windows for a vampire lair," Claire observed. "Not to mention the gap in the roof." She aimed the flashlight up to the missing ceiling. "Wouldn't they need a dark place to sleep during the day?"

"Maybe. If they took their role-playing that seriously. Maybe they sleep in the basement."

"Basement?" She shuddered beside him. "I thought New Orleans couldn't build underground because it sits below sea level," Claire whispered.

"This house has a raised basement. Most plantations did. We actually entered the house on the second floor."

"Oh, right."

The hallway was littered with trash, leaves and broken furniture. He stepped slowly, watching out for weak spots in the floor, turning left into a room that had once been a parlor, but had been converted a century ago or more into an office.

The room was empty now except for sagging bookshelves and a three-legged chair lying on its side. A door leading from the office led into a smaller, darker room, probably used for storage. Rafe motioned for Claire to shine the flashlight in there, just so they could say they'd checked every room, but it was empty.

He retraced his steps and crossed the main hall, trusting Claire to follow and light the way. He could feel her at his back, hear her breathing. The next step he took he kicked a heap of something and dozens of squealing rats scratched over his boots and between his legs, scurrying every which way.

Claire screamed and dropped the flashlight, which went bumping and rolling across the floor. The light bounced off the walls and ceiling. She clutched both her arms around him as she danced and hopped trying to dodge the rodents.

As Claire stilled and the house settled back into silence, he realized he'd taken her in his arms and her face was buried in his neck. One hand rubbed her back and the other was tangled in her hair. The locks were so soft between his fingers and he found himself stroking the curly strands. He inhaled, smelling her honey shampoo and his body reacted.

Great time for this, Moreau.

"Are you all right?"

She sniffed and nodded, but her body still trembled. Neither of them moved.

"It was just a nest of rodents. They were more scared of us than we were of them." He continued rubbing her back and stroking her hair. He could get used to this playing-the-hero thing.

"Speak for yourself." Her voice sounded so timid. "You weren't scared."

"Sure I was. For a second there."

She lifted her head. "You were not." He could feel her grin more than see it, since the flashlight was lying some feet away and pointed in the opposite direction. But her smile faded as he watched her mouth and lowered his to kiss her.

What the hell? He pulled back, dropped his arms and strode over to pick up the flashlight. He *had* lost his edge if all he wanted was to take her right there against the grimy wall.

"Come on." He shone the light into the room, which had clearly been a waiting area with chairs lining two walls. He took her hand and headed down the main hall past the staircase, then hesitated at the door on the right.

From the corner of his eye, he caught a glimpse of light flickering from beneath a door two down on the left.

Turning to Claire, he pointed at the door, put his finger to his lips and clicked off the flashlight, plunging them into blinding darkness. Which was stupid, come to think of it. Any element of surprise they might have had had disappeared when they'd disturbed the rats' nest and Claire screamed.

Rafe gave the flashlight to Claire, drew his Sig and then slowly made his way down the hall to the door with the light underneath. In the darkness, Rafe reached behind him and Claire's hand found his. He squeezed it, not sure if it was in reassurance or warning. Or both. The air seemed to grow colder, except for Claire's warm breath on his neck.

Gingerly, he turned the crystal doorknob. As if a movie soundtrack had provided it, the door hinges screeched, sounding strident in the utter silence.

As the door was opened wider, light from dozens of candles seeped into the dark hallway.

Rafe blinked as his eyes adjusted. Ten, maybe twelve people lounged on sofas, pillows and chairs, the furnishings new, the room clean. Candelabras sat on tables and hung from wall plaques.

And the people? Mostly naked and writhing in each others' arms, some blatantly having sex, some sharing oral sex and some threesomes, all enjoying each other.

A tall, lanky figure lying in a chaise longue wearing a white flowing robe open down the front petted the head of the woman kneeling at his feet and looked up at Rafe and Claire. "Do you really think your silly little gun can hurt us? Put it away," he said in a smooth French accent as he waved a languid hand with long, black pointed fingernails.

"I'll keep it out for now, thanks." Rafe stepped into the room, eyeing the group, but the few that even bothered to stop what they were doing only glanced at him in curiosity. Even the woman at Frenchie's feet laid her head down on his lap with a dreamy smile.

"You guys call yourselves The Colony?" Rafe asked the Frenchman.

The guy who'd spoken had long white hair hanging below his shoulders.

Silence was his only answer, until… "We *are* The Colony." The Frenchman, obviously their leader, pierced Rafe with a glare from eyes the color of liquid gold. "I am Armand. And you are?" He resumed petting the hair of the woman waiting at his feet. She raised her head and stared up at him adoringly.

"Rafe Moreau. And this is—" He turned to gesture to Claire. She gasped and covered her mouth with her empty hand. Her eyes filled with tears.

For the first time Rafe took a close look at the woman at Armand's feet. She wore a sheer white negligee that revealed a pert figure, her blond hair was midlength and as she turned to look at him, he noticed her big blue eyes which widened as they moved to gaze behind him.

"Claire?"

9

THE OTHER CULT FOLLOWERS eerily stopped what they were doing and turned to stare at Claire. Rafe scanned the poor pale freaks for any sign of attack, glad of the Sig in his hand.

"Oh, Julia." Claire moaned her friend's name, her tone somewhere between disillusionment and horror. "Have you been here, living like this, the whole time?"

Julia shrugged and scratched her arms, her gaze unfocused. "How long has it been?"

Rafe blinked as he watched Claire lift that horrible crocheted thing off over her head. It got caught in her glasses, and the harder she struggled to work it loose, the worse it seemed to tangle, and the more frantic she became.

He still couldn't believe how her nerdy fumbling made him feel…protective.

"Here." He stuck his Sig into his waistband, shrugged out of his jacket and strode across the room to throw it over Julia's shoulders. He even managed to not stare at the petite blonde while he did so.

And since when did he not take the chance to ogle a nearly naked woman?

"Thank you." Claire squinted at him with a wobbly smile.

And there she went making him feel all important again. Like she needed him.

It was dangerous to be needed.

She yanked the crocheted thing down over her head, and straightened her glasses, smoothing the earpieces behind her ears. "Julia, do you know what you've put me through the past four days looking for you? Worrying my head off?"

Julia's lips thinned and her wild eyes sparked. "I'm sorry, hon. I—" She frowned. Looked confused. "I figured you'd just leave. Go back to your important job. That's all you care about, anyway," she whined. "I had to beg you to take this trip with me. A-and I wanted to stay longer, but no, you had to get back."

"Julia." Claire stepped forward. "That's not it. It—" She glanced at Rafe and lowered her voice. "It just seems like all you want to do when we get together anymore is hook up with some guy. And you either want me to do the same or you leave me all alone."

"But that's because you never want to have fun."

"Fun? Picking up strangers and disappearing is not my idea of fun."

Julia flinched and then her face crumbled. "You've

changed, Claire. You were my best friend. I thought we were a family. But you don't care about me!" She ended her tirade on a sob, tears rolling down her cheeks.

"Oh, Julia, that's not true." She opened her arms, but Julia turned her face into Armand's lap and he wrapped his arms around her protectively.

Claire frowned. Rafe could see the hurt and bewilderment in her expression. That's what happened when you got involved with other people. Things got messy. Complicated. He could've told her that's why he didn't. He sure as hell wouldn't let himself care about someone the way Claire cared about Julia.

But then Claire seemed to regroup, folding her arms across her chest. "If I didn't care about you, I wouldn't have spent the last four days searching for you."

Julia lifted her head and sniffed. "When Shadow brought me to The Colony, Armand took me in, made me feel like I belonged somewhere again." Her eyes lit up and she glanced back at the white-haired guy. "And I fell in love."

"And you couldn't be bothered to call and let me know what happened to you? I thought you'd been abducted, raped, murdered!"

Julia got to her feet, her mouth a petulant pout, and closed the distance between her and Claire. "Shadow stole my phone. He took my purse and everything in it." Her face cleared and became dreamy. "But we of The Colony don't need material things to be happy." She flashed a brilliant smile. "Oh, Claire, I'm in love!"

Julia's dreamy-eyed smile was a bit too manic to be believed. Then she dived back into a sulk. "But you wouldn't understand."

"What does that mean?" Claire's brows lowered. "You don't think I'm capable of falling in love?"

Julia giggled. "With your microbes, maybe." Armand laughed and everyone in the room followed suit.

Claire's mouth dropped open and she blinked a couple times. Rafe fought the urge to go to her and put his arm around her. To tell the selfish little blonde just how passionate Claire could be under her eccentric outfits. But this wasn't his fight.

Julia's wild gaze shifted to him, slithering over him from shoulders to zipper. Lingering on the zipper. "Or maybe you *have* found someone?"

"What?" Claire glanced from Julia to him and back to Julia, her expression feigning innocence. "He's not— He's only helping me because I blackmailed him into it."

Rafe's stomach clenched. Really? Did she actually believe he'd go to this much trouble just to avoid a few questions from the cops?

Damn. Why the hell *was* he doing this? He couldn't think of any other living person he'd have done all this for. Maybe he just wanted this whole fiasco over with. The sooner he found Julia, the sooner Claire went home. But that reasoning didn't sit right in his gut.

"Poor Claire," Julia said softly. "I can only hope someday you find what Armand and I have." She gazed lovingly at Armand.

Rafe felt queasy.

Armand—his name was probably as fake as his French accent—rose from the chaise, sauntered over and draped an arm around Julia's shoulders. "After tomorrow night, Julia will truly be one of us."

"Yes." Julia turned in Armand's arms. "I'll be joined with my true family." She lifted her face to him, and they kissed. Her hair fell back, exposing red puncture marks on her neck. Looked like the rumors were true. Armand was one sick weirdo.

Claire gasped. "Have you let him cut you with something and drink your blood? Have you drunk his?"

Julia turned a brilliant smile on Claire. "I haven't drunk his yet. We're saving that for the ceremony tomorrow night. Armand is going to make me immortal like him."

"Oh, no," Claire muttered. "Julia, this isn't real. These people aren't really vampires. You know there's no such thing. I want you to come home with me right now." Claire's voice shook. "Please."

Julia barely acknowledged Claire's words as she continued to gaze into Armand's eyes. "Go home, Claire. Go back to your job at the lab and all the important work you do and leave me alone. You could never understand."

Rafe didn't know what Julia was like normally, but she was on something. Her eyes were red-rimmed, her skin pale and noticeably clammy. And she was sniffing every few seconds.

Was Armand drugging her to keep her delusional? Or was Julia taking something of her own free will?

What did it matter? There wasn't a thing he could do about any of it. Even if he wanted to. Which he didn't. He'd done his part and found the stupid bimbo. Now Claire would go home, and he'd get his life back.

"I'm not leaving you." Claire stepped forward and tried to take Julia's arm.

Armand wrenched Julia away and hissed—he actually bared his artificial fangs and hissed—at Claire.

She reared back, but Rafe was between them before he'd even realized he'd moved, his hand wrapped around Armand's throat, cutting off his air. "Give me a reason."

Armand choked, prying at Rafe's fingers, trying to pull them away.

A soft hand touched his arm. "It's okay, Rafe."

Tightening his grip in warning, he released the jerk. "Let's go, Claire." He took her arm.

He expected her to argue, to cry or threaten him. But her features flattened. "Get your coat back." She retreated to the door and snapped on the flashlight.

Her cold acceptance bothered him more than her earlier emotional pleas.

Still pressed against Armand's chest, Julia wiggled out of his jacket and extended it to him on the end of her fingers.

Rafe took it and strode over to where Claire was waiting at the door. "Ready?"

At her nod, he took the flashlight, and stepped out into the dark hallway.

CLAIRE STARED OUT THE window of Rafe's car. Her eyes stung and a tight knot of emotion was lodged in her throat. How long had Julia resented her? Had she truly been such a horrible friend? Had Julia felt abandoned when she'd gone off to college?

But the worst part of all of it was that she'd been so clueless. Now that she thought about it, the signs were there. Julia had always been boy crazy. Anytime some guy gave her the least bit of attention, she'd jump into a relationship and cling to the man as if she would drown without him.

Julia had been an easy mark for someone like Armand. He'd taken advantage of her feelings of insecurity, tempted her with some illegal substance and convinced her that her family and friends didn't care about her.

But she and Julia had faced too much adversity together, been there for each other when it really counted for something like this to destroy their lifelong friendship. Claire couldn't abandon her now.

The way she'd looked tonight, unkempt and sickly, really worried Claire. If Julia actually drank that freak's blood who knew what diseases she might contract? Even without the ceremony being imminent, the sooner she got Julia away, the better.

But she couldn't involve Rafe any further. Who knew how dangerous those creeps would get if they were threatened or thwarted? Or how far Rafe might go if the situation escalated? He'd almost choked Armand back there.

In that moment, Claire had lost a piece of her heart to him. Surely no rational woman could experience those kinds of heroics and not fall a little in love. Which would've worried her more, except she'd read somewhere that going through a highly emotional experience with someone produced false feelings of closeness—even love. But she did owe him a lot.

Claire glanced at him for the first time since leaving the asylum. His jaw was set and his eyes were narrow slits. She longed to reach over and cup his tight jaw in her palm. To run her fingers through his silky black hair. Even lean in and press her lips to the corner of his oh-so-expressive mouth.

"Thank you for…everything."

Rafe shrugged, nodded.

Hey, that was progress. He'd actually let her thank him.

He stomped on the clutch and jerked the gearshift, downshifting to exit the freeway. He was taking her back to his place. But she should get her things and go to a hotel tonight.

Shadow had more than likely—as she'd suspected— taken Julia's room key to get in and steal her things, so she should be safe in a different hotel tonight. There really was no reason to ever see Rafe again.

She resisted pressing a palm to the ache in her chest. Drew a deep breath and held it, shoving the depression back down, bricking it in behind a wall of common sense. This was merely that emotion derived from mutually experienced danger.

Rafe glanced at her as he came to an intersection somewhere in the French Quarter. "You okay?"

She nodded and let out a long breath. "I'm fine." Then she closed her eyes to avoid any further discussion.

When she opened them he was turning into the parking lot behind Once Bitten. Rafe glanced at her with a wary look as he parked the car and turned off the engine.

She managed a weak smile. "I'll be okay."

With an accepting shrug, he jumped out and headed for the stairs. Claire sighed, climbed out at a much slower pace and trudged up behind him.

Once inside Rafe's apartment, she stood awkwardly at the door. She should call a cab to take her to a hotel.

Rafe stood at the table, his laptop open, typing in— she assumed—his password. "You can use this to check for flights home. I'm going to relieve Ro at the bar." He headed for the joining staircase, but stopped and faced her. "Shadow is still out there. Feel free to sleep here. I'll be working the rest of the night, anyway."

Before Claire could think what to say, he was headed downstairs, the door closed behind him.

She blinked. Looked around the room. The reality of her situation began to penetrate. He expected her to return to Boston. And why shouldn't he? He'd found Julia.

She wasn't returning to Boston, of course.

With that thought, she concentrated on the problem of Julia and the cult. She needed to formulate a plan. And she needed to make a list. Yes. She grabbed her purse and dug around for her little notebook with the pen attached.

Making lists always made the overwhelming seem possible. Put things in black and white so she could find a logical solution. So, how to convince Julia to leave that awful cult?

She tapped her pen on the table. Tapped some more... Maybe begin with the practical things to be done.

Call hotel—arrange for belongings to be packed and left at the concierge's desk.
Call Sergeant Mulroney—suggest someone to hire.
A cult specialist? Is there such a thing?

If she wanted to stop Julia from drinking that jerk's blood, he only had until tomorrow to find a solution. Better start by calling the sergeant. Even at this late hour, he picked up on the first ring and she filled him in on their success in finding Julia. As expected, Mulroney told her there was nothing to be done since Julia was an adult and was staying of her own free will.

However, he recommended a security firm that might be able to help. It was run by a group of ex-military personnel who provided tactical rescue of kidnap victims.

Before she hung up, she made sure he knew Rafe and Once Bitten had nothing to do with Julia's disappearance or the cult. That seemed the least she could do for the man who had put his life at risk for her. More than once.

What would it be like to have that kind of man in one's life all the time?

Stick to the matter at hand, Claire.

Trying not to get her hopes up, she called the twenty-four-hour hotline for the security firm and explained her situation. Although nothing about forcibly removing Julia was specifically mentioned, Claire was given the impression that extraction was a service they might provide. Unfortunately they were based in L.A. and the soonest they could help in a non-life-threatening situation was three weeks.

Claire had twenty hours. If that.

She closed her phone and laid it on the table. She'd just have to rescue Julia herself. If she could get her away from Armand's influence maybe she could talk some sense into her. But she'd need to go during the day and hope Armand was asleep. If Julia was too delusional to listen to reason, then she'd have to try forcing her out to the cab.

Claire took off her glasses and pinched her nose. There was no one to help her now. She was alone.

Back in Boston, she was accustomed to being alone. And at twenty-nine, with no one special in her life, she'd pretty much accepted that she might be alone the rest of her life. But that was before Rafe had shown her what she was capable of.

Could she go on with her life never feeling his touch, or hearing his soft Southern drawl ever again? She'd have to.

Her future loomed before her. Lonely. Empty. Filled with what-ifs. Straightening her spine, she grabbed her glasses from the table. Self-pity wouldn't save Julia.

After a long hot shower, she wrapped a towel around her and padded out to her overnight bag. The room was mostly dark, the only light coming from the weak bulb in the bathroom. Street noise outside had quieted.

She retrieved her still-folded PJs and recalled why she hadn't worn them the night before. Memories of the things Rafe had done to her, with her, sent a shockwave of desire pulsing between her thighs. The feel of his hands on her body. His mouth. She shivered, dropped the towel and clasped her breasts, rubbing her thumbs over the tightening nipples. As she slid her hand down between her thighs, a shadow in the corner moved.

She gasped and covered herself with her arms.

A man sat in a chair at the table. She could feel his gaze on her like a buzz of electrical current. Her heart thumped in her chest and she couldn't catch her breath. "Rafe?"

10

Rafe hadn't meant to come up here. He should be pouring drinks at the bar. Or working on payroll.

But Claire was leaving. And he wanted one more taste of her. It was as simple—and as messed up—as that. And, oh, when she'd dropped that towel.

"Come over here, *cher.*"

She hesitated, and then took a few steps toward him until she was a couple feet away. She was trembling, and so close he could feel her heat and smell her clean linen and honey scent. Impossibly, his body hardened even more.

"Don't cover yourself, not from me."

She blinked and didn't move. Would she refuse him? Then she let her arms drop to her sides.

He groaned. Her breasts were full and ripe, the nipples so tight and pointed, as if they were begging to be touched.

"Now take the towel from your hair."

He watched her chest rise as she drew in a shaky breath, lifted her arms to pull the towel away and then dropped it on the floor. Her hair spilled down around her shoulders in dark, curling mutiny.

He'd never been so hard in his life. He licked his lips. "Claire." He leaned forward to grip her waist and bring her between his thighs.

He took it as a good sign when she moaned and held on to his shoulders, so he slid his hands up and cupped the sides of her breasts. Her skin beneath his fingers. So soft. He lowered his forehead to her sternum and swallowed back need. Need for her. Her body. Her presence. In his bed. In his lonely apartment. He felt her shiver, and slid his thumbs across her nipples. Heard her quick intake of breath as they tightened to hard peaks.

His blood racing, he licked one, then rolled the other between thumb and fingers.

Her nails dug into his scalp as she cried out. Smiling, he sucked harder and swirled his tongue around the bud.

But he needed more, wanted to be inside her, with her. He tugged her closer and moved his mouth down to her belly, gently scraping with his teeth. Desperately, he helped her up to straddle his lap, unbuttoning his constricting jeans as fast as his trembling hands would let him.

While he freed his aching cock, she yanked his shirt off over his head and kissed along his jaw to his throat. Her hands roamed down his back, around his waist and up over his chest, tracing his tattoo with her fingers, thumbing his sensitive nipples.

He returned her kisses eagerly with a thrusting tongue. His hands fumbled with the protection, then he positioned his cock at her entrance. Breaking the kiss, he caught her gaze and grasped her hips to press her down over him.

He shuddered as she sank onto him and he held her still so he didn't embarrass himself before they'd even moved. He was buried deep inside her and she was hot and tight around him.

Pressing his nose to her throat, he swallowed and gritted his teeth against unwanted emotions. But he couldn't shake the goofy notion that this was where he belonged. He'd never belonged anywhere before, but he did here, with her. Surrounded by her. This woman who'd humo... Who thought he was one of the

...ped her ...l him anymore after tonight.
...nose and ...shed up with his hips. Her long
...e some- ...nd she used her leverage to rise
...shucking ...ain and again. He groaned and
...ck in bed ...he moved over him. She made
...rsued her friend: with relent-
...almed his
...her tongue ...d he let go of her waist and
...n ache. All ...n his hands, reveling in the
...iss.
...pite his ear- ...shock wave. He'd wanted

to wait for her to come, his whole body was quickly clenched in pure pleasure. Then he felt her passage grip his cock and squeeze and she stilled and arched away from him, a low keening cry rumbling in her throat.

He'd never seen or heard anything so sexy in his life. He thrust up with his hips, pulled out and pushed back in, finding his release in her, finishing with a long groan of pleasure.

When he could breathe again, he opened his eyes. His cheek lay on her breasts and her fingers ran lazily over his shoulder, down his back. He had to force his arms to relax from around her back and tried to sit up. Her arms tightened around him and she hummed her disapproval.

"Don't worry, *cher*. I'm not going anywhere." He gripped her butt and stood. Her long legs wrapped around him as he carried her to the bed and t[...]bled down with her onto the mattress.

His weight on his elbows and knees, he cu[...] face and softly kissed her lips, her forehead, eyes. After a few moments of lying with her, how found the strength to untangle himself, his jeans and underwear before crawling ba[...] beside her.

With a whimper, she reached for him, p[...] nape and brought his mouth back to hers, [...] growing bolder, sweeping in and making hi[...] of a sudden he got it. This was a goodbye k[...]

Everything in him screamed refusal. Des[...]

lier one-last-time intentions, he wasn't ready to let her go. He took control of the kiss, moving over her, caressing her flesh with his hands and following with his mouth. He licked and nibbled at her shoulder, at the sensitive place just below her ear, which made her moan.

His lips and tongue traveled down to the side of her full breast, beneath it, nuzzling all around until she purred and took his head and guided him to her nipple.

He took his time licking and sucking first one then the other, building her up slowly before moving down to her belly. He held her hips still when she tried to lift them and brought his lips to her pelvic bone and farther down through her trimmed curls to the hot wet core of her.

Without him asking, she spread her thighs and guided him to her, her fingers tensing his scalp. She writhed and whimpered while he brought her to the brink. She wanted it now, but he pulled back. If this night was all they would have he was going to make damn sure she never forgot him. So, he soothed her fever, making her wait, until she begged him to finish what he'd started.

He used every skill he had, using his tongue and fingers to bring her once more to the edge and make her plead, and then, this time he watched as she lost control and yelled his name. She dragged in long breath after long breath, as if she'd just run a marathon. Until he realized she'd started sobbing.

Merde. What had he done? As he leaped up beside

her, she rolled away from him, trying to hide her face and streams of tears.

Women. He curled around her, reached over and smoothed the hair away from her wet cheeks and tucked her head under his chin. "Shhh, now, *cher*," he murmured.

She cried harder, sobbing as if she'd been storing up tears for decades. He panicked, unsure how to help her exactly. He stroked her back and crooned, "Hush, now." And, "It's all right, *cher*."

After a few minutes she let out a deep sigh. "I'm sorry." She wiped her cheeks and he grabbed a couple tissues from the bedside table and handed them to her.

"Thank you."

"Ain't no thing, *cher*."

"It is a thing." She wiped her cheeks with the tissues. "It's everything. I guess it's all finally getting to me. The last several days of being so scared. The things Julia said. Worrying about her still." She blew her nose.

"She made her choice. The Colony's not dangerous. She'll be all right."

She gave him a skeptical look, but didn't respond. After a few minutes of silence he thought she might drift off to sleep.

"Julia's mother was never well. Bipolar, actually." Claire spoke quietly.

Rafe raised his brows, but said nothing.

"Julia used to come over every night right around dinnertime, and my mom always invited her to eat with us." Claire chuckled. "She'd always think about it for a second, and then agree to stay like she was doing us a favor." Claire sniffed and wiped her nose with the tissue. "She had such a fierce pride, despite the fact she was always filthy, her clothes were ragged and her hair so ratted, my mom finally took her to a salon and had it cut into a cute bob. I think that's when she decided she wanted to become a hairdresser."

Claire drew a deep breath and took the hand he'd left resting on her waist and twined her fingers through his. "There was no stability at Julia's mom's house. Sometimes it was okay. Mostly not. But despite Julia's tough exterior, she was always susceptible to any guy who paid her the least bit of attention. She clung to boyfriends so tight they'd end up running in the opposite direction."

Rafe let out a reluctant breath. "She's not a little girl anymore, Claire."

She stilled. "I know."

"You can't make her leave if she doesn't want to. It's her choice."

She tugged her fingers out from between his. "But she's been brainwashed."

Rafe scoffed. "Come on. She may be confused, emotional but she hasn't been brainwashed." He rose up on one elbow to look Claire in the eye. "She's there of her own free will."

"I told you, she's always been susceptible to anyone who made her feel special."

Anger seared a path to his gut. "She still chose to leave you, Claire." He rolled off the bed, shoved his legs into his jeans and paced to the kitchen. Twisting to face her, he jabbed a finger toward her. "Wake up and notice the real world. Everyone looks out for number one. You think she's worried about you? Hell, no. You saw how she treated you back there."

He pulled the coffeemaker out, began filling the carafe with water. "That's the way the world is, Claire. People leave you and you can't count on anyone but yourself. The sooner you learn that, the easier life gets."

CLAIRE BLINKED. THAT'S THE way the world was? My God, he was so bitter. Were they even talking about Julia anymore? She didn't think so. She sat up and scooted to the edge of the mattress, thinking about his words, *people leave you.* "Your parents were in a car accident, Rafe. They didn't choose to leave you."

He jerked his gaze to her, narrowed his eyes. "Right." He grabbed a can of coffee from the fridge.

She sniffed and dabbed at her nose again with the tissue. Maybe he would talk about it now. "What happened after they died? Did you have family to take you in?"

He scooped coffee grounds into the filter. "Sure. I went to live with my dear old pappy. My mother's father. After a year of that I finally understood why my mother got pregnant with me at sixteen and married my dad."

Claire swallowed. Did she really want to hear this? "Did your grandfather abuse you?"

He glanced at her, his expression cold, unrelenting. "I just got tired of being his nursemaid."

"He was sick?"

"Sick?" He scoffed. "You ever seen a man so drunk he pisses himself?" He jabbed the start button on the coffeemaker and turned his back to her, leaning his palms on the counter's edge.

"So you ran away. Lived on the streets."

He didn't answer. She stood and wrapped the sheet around herself, then moved close to him. "How did you come to own your own business?"

"Same as anyone." He smirked. "Got arrested. Swore I'd never be locked up again. Found work on an oil rig in the Gulf." He shrugged. "Saved my pennies and the rest is history."

Claire hadn't thought she could admire him any more than she did. She was wrong. "You beat the odds."

He reached for mugs from the cabinet, slammed one down at her last words. "Yeah, that's me. One in a million." His jaw tightened before he turned away from her. "And I sure as hell didn't need or want anyone's help," he ground out between clenched teeth.

A chill ran down Claire's spine. Meaning he didn't need her. But she knew that already. So why did it hurt deep in her chest? Had she really thought their love-making had been something special to him?

The coffeemaker gurgled in the otherwise silent apartment.

But she still wasn't leaving without Julia. And she

wasn't going to leave here without telling the great loner a thing or two.

"Did you know there are over thirty-thousand motor vehicle-related fatalities every year in the U.S.?"

He turned to lean his back against the counter, folded his arms and threw her a bewildered look.

"And I believe the number of alcoholics is something like twelve million."

"Where do you get this stuff?"

Yes. She was a statistics geek. "I told you. I just remember data easily." She pushed her glasses up self-consciously. "But my point is, it's illogical to take what happened to you personally."

Rafe jerked his gaze to hers. "It sure as hell felt personal."

Claire bit her lip. "Yes. You're right. I'm sorry. I—I didn't mean… That is, I only meant that we live in an imperfect, random world. The whole human race could've been one molecule away from never becoming more than an amoeba. I know it's tempting to ask oneself, Why did this bad thing happen to me? But that's like wondering why Homo sapiens lived and Homo erectus became extinct. Who knows?"

He squinted. "So everything is just chance and nothing really matters in the end?"

She frowned. "No. We all matter. *We* can make the difference. There is an indefinable quality, an unknown factor in the equation that I believe can't be understood." She mimicked him and leaned against the counter's edge beside him, adjusting the sheet around her. Her feet were cold on the linoleum floor. "It's one of the big questions humans have been struggling to answer ever since we could reason. Why do we exist? Some find comfort in a higher power. Others are always searching." She shrugged again. "But no matter what the answer, I believe we have a choice."

"About what?"

She was captured by gray eyes so intense she thought she'd never escape their scrutiny. And why would she want to? "We can choose to let what happens to us defeat us, or we can fight and make something good come from it."

"How could anything good come from what happened?"

Claire looked at him. Really looked at him. Who was *she* to try to make sense of anything? Maybe she would just make things worse. All she had—like her microbes in her lab—was the truth she'd observed. "You were left alone, to fend for yourself. Living on the fringe of so-called normal society. And yet you persevered. You've created a place for others like yourself. The people who don't fit in, the individuals that society might call freaks can come to Once Bitten and know there are others like themselves, and not feel so alone."

She realized that she'd always felt like an outcast, too. A painfully shy, socially awkward, fashionably backward nerd. But Rafe had made her see herself differently.

He stared at her, the creases of bitterness and torment between his brows and around his mouth slowly fading. He looked at her as if he were seeing her for the first time. Then he brought his hands to either side of her face, tilted it up and lowered his mouth to hers.

The kiss was gentle and full of wonder. Something deep in her belly ached for the joy of it. He pulled away, stared at her again and then took possession of her mouth with a fierceness that made her knees lose strength and her chest surge with emotion. She let go of the sheet and wrapped her arms around his neck, returning his kisses, whimpering with need.

In one swift move he scooped her up into his arms and carried her to the bed, the sheet trailing behind. Her back hit the mattress and hot male body covered her. She opened the sheet and wrapped it around his back, cocooning them both inside it, hiding from the world and all its mysteries and complications. All she cared about right now was how his skin rubbed against hers, how his body was hard where hers was soft. How the hair on his chest and legs tickled and warmed her.

He kissed her nose, her eyes, her temple, then down her jaw to her neck, his stubble rough against her sensitive throat. He used his knees to spread her thighs and slipped inside her. He groaned her name and set up a rhythm that called to the ancient female in her. She dug her fingers into his back and met him thrust for thrust, encouraging him with guttural sounds that might have been the word yes in some primal language.

And when she needed him to go faster and harder he seemed to read her mind. He obliged until she was fighting to breathe and reaching a zenith and then tumbling down, and he froze above her. Then he shuddered and gradually relaxed.

Still marveling at the phenomenon of her blinding orgasm, Claire caressed his back, his shoulders, his neck. Never again would she question whether she was frigid or unfeeling, or undersexed.

But at this moment, she couldn't imagine that any other man would make her feel this way.

11

RAFE WAS DREAMING. He was surrounded by warmth, wrapped in loving arms. He felt safe. Being held so tightly his chest felt compressed.

Then the weight on his chest shifted and a female sighed, and Rafe awoke slowly.

Claire half lay on him, her cheek on his chest, her breasts pushed against his side, her leg crossed over his. Beneath his hand her back rose and fell with her steady breathing. He smiled and felt a surreal sense of peace.

Her warm skin pressed against his as weak light filtered through the blinds. Almost morning.

He'd actually slept several hours. With someone next to him in his bed. Hearing her breathing. Feeling her warm body snuggling against his. He slid his hand up her spine and she moaned and arched, murmuring a satisfied hello.

"Hey," he muttered.

She stiffened, rose up on her elbows. "What time is

it?" Her eyes were wide, frantic. Even so, their deep brown color reminded him of the chicory coffee he loved so much.

"You have an early flight?"

"Um." She blinked. "Yes." She rolled away from him and grabbed her glasses off the bedside table. As she slipped them on, he rolled toward her and slid his arm around her waist.

"Cher." He pressed a soft kiss to the small of her back and began nibbling his way to her hip. "Stay today, I'll take you to the airport tomorrow."

She covered his hand with hers and squeezed. "I—I can't."

A sharp pain lodged somewhere between his throat and chest. And she…shot off the bed and into the bathroom as if she couldn't wait to put as much distance between them as possible. Evidently she wasn't feeling the same warmth.

Last night he'd practically opened a vein for the woman. He never talked about his past. But he'd thought they'd…connected.

He stretched and ran a hand along his unshaven jaw. What the hell was he thinking? Had he thought he might actually get involved with her? As in…a relationship?

Who'd have guessed it? Raphael Moreau, the king of the tourist fling, had feelings for a woman. How had that happened? How could he have been so stupid? The woman lived in Boston. She had a PhD, for crying out loud. This was good that she was leaving. She'd disrupted his life enough already.

He crawled out of bed and padded to the bathroom, knocked on the door she'd closed. "Claire?"

"Just a sec."

"Claire, give me a few minutes to shower and shave and I'll take you to the airport."

Silence.

He knocked again. "Claire."

The door opened and she emerged fully dressed. "Thank you, but I need to go now." She crossed to the table and slung her purse up onto her shoulder.

"*Cher.* There's no way you can get a cab here before I get out of the shower. Give me ten minutes." He spun toward the bathroom.

"No!"

He turned back.

She closed her eyes and pushed her glasses up on her nose. "What I mean is, I arranged for a cab to be here this morning when I booked my flight last night." She gave him a smile so false a blind man could've seen through it. "Thank you for everything." She extended her right hand.

What the—? He glared at her. A stupid handshake? After last night? Well, fine. If she wanted to pretend there was just sex between them, he could do that. He damn sure could do that. He clasped her hand, raised it to his lips. "Take care, *cher.*" Dropping her hand, he gave her his back as he headed into the bathroom, closed the door and turned on the shower.

CLAIRE BIT HER LIP, HARD, as she made her way down the outside stairs of Rafe's apartment. She refused to cry, but her stupid vision was blurry even with her glasses on. Digging in her purse for her cell phone to call a cab, she stood at the base of the stairs, wishing she really had thought to arrange for a cab to pick her up.

"You're up early."

Claire jumped and spun to look behind her, her heart rate tripled.

Ro leaned against the back door to the bar, smoking a cigarette under the stairs.

"Ro, you scared me." Claire tried to catch her breath.

"It's Rowena." As she blew a stream of smoke from her mouth, Rowena raised a brow, threw her cigarette down and ground it out with her boot. "You have a good time last night?" Her gaze traveled up the stairs to Rafe's apartment door and back down again.

For the briefest instant Claire thought she saw pain in the woman's eyes. She certainly didn't blame Rowena if she'd had to work all night because Rafe had been... preoccupied with Claire. She suddenly felt embarrassed. "Have you been here all night?" She tried to smile.

Rowena shrugged. "Sometimes that's the way it goes."

"I'm—I'm sorry."

Rowena raised a disbelieving brow. "Where you going?"

"To the airport." She held up her cell. "I was just calling a cab."

Now both brows rose. "And Rafe knows you're leaving New Orleans?"

Claire nodded. "Yes, of course."

"Cool. I'll take you." She dug a key from her jeans pocket as she strode toward a pale yellow pickup.

"No, that's okay. I'm sure you're exhausted." Now what was she going to do?

"No, really." She narrowed her eyes. "I want to."

Claire scanned the small gravel parking lot as if she'd find an answer there. What reason could she possibly give Ro for not wanting her to give her a ride to the airport? "I, uh…"

"You're not really going to the airport, are you?"

"Um… Please don't tell Rafe. But I have to try to get my friend away from that cult."

Rowena cocked her head, speculation in her eyes. "And you're not going home until you succeed?"

Claire lifted her chin. "No."

"Then I should tell you. Someone came in last night with a message for you."

"For me?" Claire didn't know anyone in the area except Sergeant Mulroney. "Was it a policeman?"

"No. He was a vamp. He said to tell you that Julia will meet you at the St. Luis cemetery as soon as possible."

Joy spilt over Claire. "Julia? Oh, Rowena, that's so wonderful. Thank you!" She opened her cell and brought up the cab company's number. Julia must have sobered up by this morning and realized the danger she was in.

"Come on. I'll still give you a ride," Rowena offered. "It'll be faster than waiting for a cab."

She wanted to ask why Rowena hadn't told her this earlier, but she was too anxious to get to Julia. "If you're sure you don't mind. That'd be great."

Before she even thought about the sergeant or collecting her things from Les Chambres Royale, she was barreling down the mostly empty streets of the French Quarter in Rowena's beat-up pickup. It was a good thing Rowena knew where they were going because Claire was so turned around she wasn't sure if even the tourist's map she had tucked in her purse would've helped. She'd always been directionally challenged.

"Here you go." Rowena pulled up outside the ornate iron gates of the cemetery and shifted the truck into Park. "Do you want me to wait?"

Claire checked her cell reception. Only one bar. Hmm. "Would you mind? I'm not sure I can call a cab from here."

"Sure. Maybe I can help with your friend."

"Oh, that'd be great." Maybe Julia would listen to Rowena. Even in civilian clothes Rowena stood out. Her heavy black eyeliner and lipstick made the jeans and sweater she had on this morning seem out of place. No sleek floor-length black gown a la Morticia Addams today.

But the jeans were much more practical for tromping around a weed-infested cemetery. Rowena followed Claire through the entryway.

Aboveground graves framed by stone and plaster about three feet high were surrounded by short iron fences, marked with marble statues of Mary, or St. Francis, or a crucifix. But as she walked farther, graves gave way to wall crypts stacked four and five coffin-size squares high. Then came rows of barrel-vaulted and pitched-roof stone crypts. Built so close together, with parapets and steps leading up to a doorway, they looked like tiny houses.

Some had family names carved in the stone above the doorway, or other elaborate bas relief carvings, some had urns and vases of flowers on stoops in front of the entryways, and some roofs sported stone crosses on a spire like a church.

"Julia!" Claire called out every couple of minutes. Was she not here? Maybe they'd tracked her down and taken her back to the asylum.

Claire clenched her hands into fists, envisioning Armand dragging Julia away, forcing her to go through with that ceremony against her will. She could practically feel the satisfaction of smacking Armand in the face.

And since when did she condone violence of any

kind, much less imagine enjoying it? She needed to get back to Boston and her normal life as soon as possible.

Her days might be predictable, boring even, but at least there she didn't have to experience danger, and heartache, and—and passion. And the exquisite sensations of lovemaking, and the thrill of having a man like Rafe Moreau look at her and really see her and want her....

Why on earth did she want to return to her lonely life in Boston?

She chose a row of wall crypts at random and turned, then realized she could get lost amid all the similar-looking walls and never find her way back. Wait. Rowena was missing, too. Returning to the main aisle, she called out, "Rowena?" She scanned the aisles she could see. "Rowena?" she yelled louder.

She better find a point of reference or she'd be wandering around lost out here forever.

There. A miniature dome twenty feet in the sky with a pair of angels sitting atop it. The dome was perched on four columns that sat on the pitched roof of a multi-vault crypt. She took note of its position relative to hers and the entrance gate, and then headed farther into the cemetery calling Julia's and Rowena's names over and over.

"Claire! Over here!" It was Rowena and she sounded panicked.

Claire started running toward the sound of Rowena's voice and finally spotted her in the doorway of a pitched-roof crypt. How had she gotten the door open?

And why? Julia was inside the crypt? Hurt? Overdosed? Claire's emotions kicked into overdrive as she pictured her friend hurt or dead because she'd tried to escape. *Oh, Julia.*

She rushed past Rowena into the cool, gloomy crypt, but couldn't see a thing until her eyes adjusted to the dark. Just as she realized the crypt was empty, the door slammed shut behind her. She spun around and shoved on the door. "Rowena?" But the door didn't budge. There was no latch on this side. Why would there be? She shoved on the door again, this time throwing her whole body into it. "Rowena! Let me out!"

No one answered. Claire rubbed her shoulder where she'd hit the door. She stood there, stunned. Surely this wasn't happening. Really? How could she have fallen for such a clichéd trick? But then, how could she have known Rowena would do something so completely over-the-top crazy?

Sighing, she grabbed her cell phone from her purse, but now it didn't even show one bar. Not surprising inside this thick stone tomb. She shuddered. No one knew she was here. She could be trapped for days, weeks....

Stop it. Panicking would solve nothing. She must find a way to get out of here on her own.

The crypt wasn't completely dark or she wouldn't be able to see her hand in front of her face. She followed the source of light to several holes in the crumbling blackened brick wall. The openings were along the top of the wall, maybe seven feet high. Could she bust more of the stone away and fit through? Even if she could, how would she climb up to them?

Her only hope was the door, then. She'd have to find something to bang it with. Spinning around, she began searching the tomb for anything large enough to break down the door. Her prospects did not seem hopeful.

By the time Rafe got out of the shower and headed downstairs to catch up on all the work he'd missed lately, he'd almost convinced himself he was glad Claire was out of his life. She was nothing but a pain in his backside. Good for a couple nights of fun, like any other vacation fling.

Then he realized he was pouring himself a tumbler of vodka at nine-thirty in the morning. Pappy used to drink vodka for breakfast…

He cursed long and loud, pitched the tumbler across the empty bar and savored the satisfaction of the glass shattering against the steel cage hanging from the ceiling.

So he'd wanted a couple more days with her. Maybe that would've been all it took to get her out of his system. Maybe not. In less than a week, she'd managed to insert herself into the very core of his life.

He stalked to his office and sat at his desk. Flipped open his accounts payable and turned on his calculator. The rows of numbers reminded him of all the statistics she'd quoted him. He smiled, thinking about her adjusting her glasses, or how she would bite her thumbnail….

He pictured her when he'd first seen her, so out of her element, stuttering, but refusing to take no for an answer. And never giving up the search for her friend, even when the odds were stacked against her. And how she'd stood up to Armand.

If she was that relentless when trying to save a friend, how would she be with someone she'd promised herself to 'til death do them part? Would she never leave them? Never give up on them?

He'd never had anyone like that in his life.

Work, Moreau. This bar is your life.

If he couldn't look at numbers right now, he'd count inventory. He shoved away from his desk and stalked to the storeroom. He had an order of bourbon due. And boxes of rum to unload. And he needed fresh fruit for garnishes. Maybe some fresh strawberries for daiquiris....

No!

Claire was probably on her way to Boston by now. She wouldn't be ordering anymore strawberry daiquiris. He refused to think about her. It was over. She was no longer his problem. This bar was. And if he didn't give one hundred percent to his business, he could lose it.

He grabbed up the box cutter and began unpacking bottles. He'd be damned before he let anything else be taken from him.

12

THE TOMB WAS COLD. This might be the Deep South, but it was still February. The sunny morning had clouded over and Claire heard thunder rumbling in the distance. The walls were clammy and the air was getting chillier by the hour.

According to her cell, it was almost eleven. Claire had been pounding on the door and shouting for close to two hours. Her throat was raw, her voice was almost gone and her hands were sore. With her back to the door, she slid down the door, and dropped her forehead to her knees. At least she had her poncho with her.

As if to torment her, she thought she heard someone talking far in the distance. She stopped breathing, held very still and cocked her head. There was the rustle of leaves in the biting wind. The roar of traffic across town. But no human voices.

How cruel. Was she losing her sanity or had someone's voice simply carried farther on the wind? She dropped her head again.

Then raised it. There it was again. A woman's voice. A little closer now. Saying something about the eighteenth century. The woman's words grew more distinct, louder now. She was describing the difference between a box tomb and a ledger stone. A tour guide? A cemetery tour!

Claire scrambled up and pounded on the door. "Hello? Help me!" she screamed. "Hello, can anyone hear me?" She repeated the words, and then listened. The woman's voice was gone.

But a different voice floated through the hole in the crumbling bricks. "Hello?" It sounded like an adolescent, with enough of a touch of huskiness to be a boy.

She darted from the door to the wall and jumped and shouted as her mouth got close to the opening. "Help." Another jump. "Hello." Another jump. "Help me." Her voice was going. She rubbed her throat and waited.

The young teen shouted to a friend. "Hey, man, I heard something in that grave."

A second male teen voice said, "Yeah, sure. You think I'm gonna fall for that old trick?"

"No!" She jumped and yelled but no sound came out. She tried again. "It's not a trick. I'm trapped inside! Please!" Her voice gave out on the last word and it sounded more like a croak. She waited and listened.

The second teen scoffed, "The tour guide is leaving us behind. There ain't no one in there."

"I swear, I thought I heard something."

Their voices faded into the distance.

Her shoulders drooped. Why hadn't she thought of a tour group coming? Then she could've saved her voice. But if there was one tour group, surely there'd be another coming by in an hour or so. And she needed to get her voice back for when they did. She needed water. Or the closest thing to.

Of course!

She dug in her purse, certain she had at least a breath mint or a piece of gum.

Jackpot! A granola bar! And a small bottle of water from the airplane, half full. And gum. And mints. She smiled, feeling as if she'd stumbled upon Aladdin's cave with all its treasures.

She sat and ate the granola bar and sipped at the water, reserving it to make it last longer, just in case. Then chewed a piece of gum, willing her voice to heal.

She finally checked her cell phone for the time and realized it was already past noon. If the tours didn't run every hour, hopefully they ran every two hours. What else was in her purse that she could use?

She sat in the small spot where the sunlight shone, rummaging around in her tote. Notepad and pen! Of course! She wrote *Trapped in tomb, Please help!* on a piece of notepaper and tried to slip the paper through the thin crack in the door. But it wouldn't go no matter how she wiggled. Great. The wall was falling to pieces, but the door was airtight.

She tried jumping and tossing the note through the hole in the crumbled-out bricks, but unless she crumpled up the paper into a ball it only fluttered back down inside.

Hopefully the next tour would come by soon.

Giving up for the moment, she found a small rock and drew in the sandy dust, playing with a mathematical formula that had stumped her since college. Sometimes she'd try to solve it when she was waiting on test results in her lab.

After another hour had passed and she still heard no sounds of a tour, panic threatened, but she pushed it away. Positive thoughts would serve her best in this situation.

After another hour, emotions began to rear their ugly head, and then she heard it. Barely audible, a woman's voice, the same woman, Claire thought, talking about the same stones in the cemetery. As the voice grew slightly louder, Claire jumped to her feet and banged and banged on the door with the flat of her hands and called out for help.

Then she darted to the opening in the crumbled brick and jumped again, waiting until her voice was exactly at the opening when she shouted. She jumped and shouted and jumped and shouted, repeating it until she couldn't hear the woman's voice anymore.

As she jumped the last time her foot landed half on a pile of crumbled brick and her left ankle turned. She fell hard onto her side, catching herself on her elbow and wrist.

Claire didn't move as she strained to hear an answer.

But no one responded. This group didn't seem to have straying teens, or straying anyone.

"No!" As she tried to scramble to her feet, her ankle throbbed in sharp agony. She half crawled, half pulled herself along the chalky floor until she reached the door. Panicked, she pounded on the door until her muscles ached.

Her teeth chattered and her body shook. She examined her ankle, testing its movement. Judging from the way it felt, she was fairly certain it wasn't broken, just a bad sprain. But there was no way she could put her weight on it.

She let out a breath she'd been holding tightly along with every hope and positive thought she had left within her.

What if she really was trapped in here for days? Or even longer? What if no one ever found her? An infuriating sob escaped. She hated this place! Oh, why did Julia have to choose this crazy city in which to disappear and join a cult? Maybe she should've just left Julia here and gone home!

But this city, with its lush history and vibrant colors, its pulsing energy and unique flavors that filled the very air one breathed, this city worked a magic, a kind of voodoo on her that pulled her in and tempted her to bare her soul and believe she was someone more than she thought she ever could be. And she wasn't sure she could ever go back to being the old Claire. New Orleans had made her believe in the ghost of possibilities and in a vampire bar owner who could whisk her away to a fantasy world of passion and romance.

This city had robbed her of rational judgment.

She drew a deep breath and closed her eyes. *You are Claire Brooks of Springfield, Missouri. Scientist. Pragmatist. Realist.*

Logic and common sense had always been her allies. *Think, Claire.*

But she couldn't concentrate.

She sat up, grabbed a half broken brick and pitched it with all her might at the other side of the tomb.

Screw rationale. Screw logic and staying calm. She wanted to scream and cry and bash something. She'd never lost her temper and had a tantrum before. Not in all her twenty-nine years. She swore as soon as she got out of this place she was going to. She closed her eyes and fantasized about smacking Rowena, and Armand, and even Julia for getting her into this.

And what else in life had she been missing by always being the rational one? Passion. Romance. A true fling. Not just a couple of guilt-laden nights.

So, when she was done with her tantrum, she'd see what she could do about having a torrid affair. But there was no one back in Boston she could even remotely imagine having steamy, uninhibited sex with. In fact… the only man she wanted was Rafe.

But she'd burned that bridge with her behavior this morning. Oh, how she wished she'd appreciated what she had when she had it. She closed her eyes and relived every moment she'd had with Rafe Moreau.

WHEN RAFE HEARD THE dead bolt unlock and the door open and close, he checked his watch. Four o'clock. "Ro?" he called out, assuming she was here for her shift.

"Yeah?" Ro poked her head in his office door, her gaze darting around as if she were looking for something. "Is…everything okay?"

She must be exhausted after working back-to-back twelve-hour shifts. "Everything's caught up. I'm not going anywhere, so if you want to take some time off, I can handle things tonight."

"Time off isn't what I need." Ro stepped into the doorway and leaned her shoulder blades against the frame, raising one foot behind her. One high-heeled foot. She wore a black mini-dress that plunged so deep in the front she couldn't have a bra on. Not that she needed one, she was fairly small-breasted. But she also wore black leather high-heeled boots that came up to her mid-thigh.

"You seeing someone after work?" He shouldn't ask about her personal life. He didn't appreciate when she pried into his. They'd had a thing a few years ago when he'd first hired her on as assistant manager. It had lasted a week or so and then every once in a while one of them would need an itch scratched. It'd never been more than that for either of them, and it hadn't happened in a long while. But this look was different for her. She'd removed most of the rings from her lip and brow. It made her look softer.

"If I was seeing someone else, would you be jealous?"

Rafe frowned. What the heck was she talking about? "Uh…"

She pushed off the door frame, closed the distance between them and bent to trap him in his chair. "We got a quick half hour before Bulldog gets here." She licked her lips and moved her hands to unbutton his jeans.

He gripped her wrists and lifted her hands away. He looked into her hazel eyes and knew he'd never sleep with her again. It just wasn't right anymore. But how did he say this? He sighed. "It's not going to work anymore, Ro."

Her face hardened and her lips twisted. "I was only feeling sorry for you, anyway." She pushed away and headed for the door. "I got things to do." She sauntered off.

He almost went after her but his cell buzzed. "Moreau."

"Good afternoon, this is Les Chambres Royale Hotel calling for Ms. Claire Brooks, please."

Rafe's heart stuttered. "Ms. Brooks left town this morning."

"Oh dear, we were under the impression she was going to retrieve her luggage from us before leaving. Could you please let her know we can have them shipped to her if that would work best?"

"Are you telling me she never picked up her luggage?"

"No, sir. I mean, yes, sir, she has not claimed them."

"Did you try her cell phone?"

"Yes, sir. There was no answer. The manager said she left Once Bitten as her forwarding address."

Damn it. She might not be picking up her cell because she was on the plane, or maybe her battery died. But why would she leave town without getting her bags? Every instinct screamed that she wouldn't. Rafe ground his teeth, remembering the way she'd acted this morning. The way she had refused to even meet his gaze. And wouldn't wait to let him give her a ride to the airport.

Because she wasn't going to the airport! Because she hadn't left town. Damn it. She'd gone out to that asylum on her own to rescue Julia. Eight hours ago.

If she'd been successful, wouldn't she have gotten her luggage before heading to the airport? And if she wasn't answering her cell, it might be because Armand had taken it from her and was holding her hostage. Or worse.

He shot out of his chair, climbed the stairs to his apartment two at a time, retrieved his jacket and his gun and was halfway down the outside stairs before he remembered Ro.

He cursed under his breath and headed back into the bar.

"Ro, something's come up again." He stuck his gun in his jeans at the small of his back and shoved his arms through his jacket sleeves. "You'll be all right here?"

Ro looked up from sweeping up the glass he'd broken earlier. He allowed a twinge of guilt. But he'd make it up to her. Give her a bonus or a raise. Whatever.

"Where are you going now? I thought she'd finally left you alone."

Rafe squinted at her. She sounded pissed. More. She sounded possessive. "She's gone back to help her friend. I have to make sure she doesn't get herself hurt."

"Why?"

Ro dropped the broom, closed the distance between them and flattened her palms on his chest. "Let her get hurt if she's too stupid to know better. Why do you care?" She ran her hands over his shoulders and curled her hands around the back of his neck.

Rafe grabbed her hands and jerked them down to her sides. "Ro. She's been gone since eight this morning. She could already be hurt badly. Or being held against her will. That crazy vamp Armand said there was a special ceremony tonight to drink her friend's blood. What if they decide drinking a thimbleful isn't enough? Those Colony people aren't all playing with a full deck."

"Exactly. They could hurt you, too. Don't go, Rafe." Tears shone in Ro's eyes. "I couldn't stand it if something happened to you."

Whoa. Where had all this come from? "Look. If it will make you feel better, call the police and have them meet me at the old Delacroix asylum." He squeezed her hands. "I have to go." He turned to head for the door, but she latched onto his jacket.

"Wait!"

"Rowena, what the hell?" He circled her wrists and pulled her hands away.

She stared at him with glittering eyes full of anguish.

Did he even want to hear this?

Her face crumpled and she swung around to face away. "She's not there."

Rafe blinked. His vision blurred and the air around him seemed to evaporate. He seized Ro's shoulders and jerked her around to face him. "What are saying? How do you know?" Terror seized his chest. He shook her hard. "Ro, what did you do?"

Ro hung her head, her mascara running black streaks down her cheeks. "It's always been you and me against them," she whined. When she lifted her gaze her eyes were alight with a kind of crazy he'd never seen in them before. "I know those college sluts don't mean anything to you. And when you slept with her the first time, I figured it was just another fling. But when you left me alone again last night to go up to *her* in your apartment, I knew then that she had her claws in you and she wasn't going away. She's got you under some sort of spell, Rafe, don't you see that?"

He released his grip on her shoulders slowly and set her away from him. "You're right, Ro. I've been ignoring my business and you. But I'm back now. So you can tell me what you did to her, okay?"

"Don't patronize me!" She shoved him hard in the chest. "I'm not crazy. I just did what I had to do. For us."

Oh, no. What had Ro done? Despite his body quaking in dread, Rafe set his jaw and narrowed his eyes. "Then you better tell me what you did and where she is." He leaned close and promised retribution with his expression. "Now. Or I'll haul you into the cops and you can tell them yourself."

13

CLAIRE LIMPED AROUND the sarcophagus that sat in the middle of the tomb, testing her ankle, trying to keep it from getting stiff. The sunlight was almost gone from the hole of crumbling bricks and she knew once darkness fell completely, maneuvering around the tomb would get more difficult.

If she could use her ankle, she'd try to climb on to the sarcophagus, lean over to the hole in the wall and use the half brick she'd found to break up more bricks and enlarge the hole.

Granted, she couldn't hope to climb out of the hole, but maybe she'd get lucky and a larger part of the wall would crumble away. Although, if the entire wall fell, she could cause the tomb to collapse completely with her inside it.

At this point, with night coming on soon, and no hope of rescue anytime in the near future, that fate seemed almost preferable. Besides, moving around kept the cold at bay.

Rubbing her hands up and down the chill bumps on her arms, she took another cautious step, wincing at the pain in her ankle, but determined not to curl up and give in to panic or self-pity.

"Claire!"

She froze and held her breath like the last time she thought she'd heard a voice in the distance. *Please don't let this be a hallucination.*

"Claire, help me find you, *cher.*" The voice got louder. "Can you hear me?"

With a sob, she hobbled over to the door and pounded and shouted. "Rafe! I'm in here." She kept pounding until the door swung open and she fell out onto her hands and knees.

Then she was lifted into warm strong arms. "Claire, my God. I'm so sorry, *cher.*"

"Rafe." She held on as he ran his hands down her back and up to her shoulders.

"Are you hurt? Are you okay?"

"I t-turned my ankle and I was so s-scared and I didn't think anyone would c-come," she babbled. "And it was g-getting dark and the t-tour group didn't hear me when I yelled and yelled." She was crying and speaking incoherently, acting hysterical, she knew, but she was just so happy to be free. Was she hyperventilating?

"Breathe slowly." He was stroking her hair, her back, murmuring calming words. "It's all right now." His hands felt so comforting. She forced herself to draw in a measured breath and let it out little by little. And again.

She looked into his gray eyes, darkened with worry. "I can't believe you're here."

"Claire." His gaze dropped to her lips. For a moment she thought he might kiss her. But he drew back. "Your mouth is blue and you're shivering. We need to get you warm." He hunkered down to examine her swollen, bruised ankle, feeling the bone and muscle with gentle fingers. "This needs ice and elevation." He straightened and without asking, swung her up into his arms and carried her to his car.

In his sturdy arms she felt safe. And cared for. She rested her head on his shoulder and breathed in his masculine scent. She was no lightweight, and yet he carried her with strong steady strides over uneven ground as if she weighed no more than a microbe. He wasn't even out of breath once they reached his car.

After he set her into the passenger seat she remembered her purse and, without complaint, Rafe turned the motor on, letting it warm up before going back for her purse. When she unlocked the door, he got behind the wheel, switched on the heater and drove away, all without once glancing at her. His jaw was set, but his face was unreadable.

"How did you know where to find me?"

His body tensed and his face transformed into snarling fury. "Ro eventually confessed. I fired her. If you want to press charges, I'll back you up."

Claire was too emotional to make a rational deci-
sion about that. Part of her wanted to punch the other
woman's face to a pulp. Another part of her wanted to
curl into the fetal position and hide from the world for
a month. "Why did she do it? Is it because I took you
away from the bar so much?"

His hands tightened on the steering wheel. "She was
jealous. I thought we were friends."

She almost asked if they'd been lovers. But it was
none of her business. Still, the thought of Rafe and Rowena in bed together caused a painful jab in her chest.

"Claire, I thought she'd murdered you!" He finally
looked at her, his eyes blazing with anguish.

"I'm all right." She put her hand on his shoulder.

And then she understood. Her dying would've been
someone else that left him, in his eyes. No wonder he
was the King of Flings. If he never let himself care
about anyone too deeply, then it didn't hurt when they
left him.

And yet he'd asked her to stay this morning. And
she'd refused. How much courage had it taken for him
to even ask? He probably wouldn't again. And she didn't
blame him. She'd destroyed whatever they might've
had together.

But the important thing was, he'd come for her.

She stared out her window. "I'm not going to press
charges. I'm not permanently injured and at least she
told you what she'd done eventually."

The sun had disappeared as Rafe drove, shifting

gears with each punch of the clutch between each stop sign. Which meant that the "ceremony" was most likely about to begin. Julia could be drinking Armand's blood even now.

It also meant Once Bitten should be opening about now. "If you fired Rowena, and you're here, who's opening your bar tonight?"

His lips flatten. "Once Bitten is closed tonight."

"Oh." She squeezed her eyes closed. "I'm sorry. I've been nothing but a hassle to you."

He shot her a sizzling look, his stare intense. "That's not all you've been."

Caught in his fiery gaze, she shivered, and not just because the heat was finally thawing her toes and fingers. She wanted to crawl into his lap and kiss her way down his body. Tear off his clothes and hers and settle in for a long, passionate night with his body against hers. With his mouth and his hands, and her mouth and her hands, taking and giving pleasure until her mind was nothing but mush.

But, besides the fact that he probably couldn't wait to be rid of her, she still had to get to Julia.

He turned the car left and then a quick right into a hospital emergency room driveway.

"Oh." She'd just assumed he'd take her home. She looked at the doors swishing open and people coming out on crutches or in wheelchairs. "I don't want to go to the hospital." What she wanted was a hot cup of coffee, a hot bath and a soft bed. Preferably the same one Rafe would be in. But she'd forfeited that privilege when she'd lied to him this morning.

"Don't be ridiculous. Your ankle needs x-raying. You could be hypothermic. Dehydrated at the very least."

"My ankle is only sprained. If it were broken, I couldn't do this." She wiggled her foot around. "I had a bottle of water in my purse. And I'm not experiencing any of the symptoms of hypothermia. Shivering, slurred speech or drowsiness."

He scowled. "You should at least get checked out."

She shook her head. "I'll be fine. Could you please take me to my hotel?"

He narrowed his eyes at her. "Les Chambres Royale called me when they couldn't reach you. They still have your luggage."

Her luggage. She'd forgotten about it. She had nothing clean to change into until she retrieved it. This morning seemed like years ago. But she didn't care about clean clothes right now. "Okay, take me there, please?"

"Come on, Claire. You're still going to try to save your friend tonight, aren't you?"

She dropped her gaze to her lap. If she told him the truth, would he try to stop her? Or would he insist on going with her? She didn't want to involve him in her mess any more than she already had. If he were to get hurt because of her, she'd never have another night's peaceful sleep.

But could she lie to him again? She brought her

thumb up to her mouth and chewed on the nail. For the first time in her life she understood, deep in her bones, the phrase, *lesser of two evils*.

Yet, it was crystal clear what she couldn't do. She drew a deep breath and turned in her seat to face him. "I am going to the asylum to try to get Julia to leave the cult. But I don't want you to get involved anymore."

His eyes flared and he bared his teeth. "You are the most obstinate, pig-headed, unreasonable woman I've ever met." He yanked the car into gear and stomped on the gas. "I thought after what you must've gone through today you'd have had enough of danger. You could've died! Don't you think you've risked enough?" He drove like a wild man and cursed under his breath the whole way. "I don't know what you think you're going to accomplish with a twisted ankle. And I can't stop you if you're determined to jeopardize yourself. But I'll be damned if I'm going to help you get there," he mumbled between gritted teeth. "You can call a cab and find your own way. I have a business to run. I can't believe I was going to close the bar the whole damn night for you."

He peeled into the parking lot behind Once Bitten, slammed the gear into Neutral and pulled the brake. He jumped out and rounded the front of the car to her side. Before she could get out, he slid an arm behind her back and the other beneath her knees and lifted her into his arms, and carried her all the way up the stairs.

Claire didn't fight him. His tirade sparked a flame of warmth inside her heart. He cared about her. Maybe they could at least end this strange relationship as friends.

She wrapped her arms around his neck and kissed the underside of his jaw as he set her down to fish his keys from his pocket. With a deep groan, he turned his head and covered her mouth with his. He drew away only to unlock the door, then resumed the kiss as he swooped her up and carried her to the bed and lowered them both onto it.

Between kisses he pulled her poncho off and tossed it. She tugged his T-shirt over his head. He yanked her sweatshirt off and cupped her breast through her bra. She kissed him and unzipped his jeans. He slid his fingers under her bra straps and pushed them down her arms until her nipples were exposed, then he captured one between his lips and teased the tip with his tongue.

With a cry of delight Claire grabbed his hair and wiggled beneath him as he licked her sensitive peak. He sat up, took off his boots, found protection and slipped out of his jeans. Then he was back, covering her with his big warm body, his weight like a blanket shielding her from harm.

He helped her slide off her jeans and panties and she toed off her shoe. His fingers caressed her between her thighs while his mouth captured her nipple again. She was already aching for him when he moved between her legs and entered her with a deep thrust. He nuzzled into her neck and moved in her, setting up a rhythm that had her shouting out in pleasure within minutes.

But he stilled and waited until she came back to him, opened her eyes and smiled. Then, as she languidly kissed his stubbled jaw, he pulled out, took her waist in his hands and rolled her onto her stomach. Ready for him, she parted her thighs and he pushed in. She cried out as he filled her completely. He lay over her carefully, protectively, and laced his fingers through hers, to place her arms over her head, to build her up all over again.

The angle and depth of his strokes from this position had Claire calling out for Rafe, begging for completion. But he was relentless, kissing along her neck, nibbling her ear, gently biting her shoulder. Whispering other things he wanted to do to her, with her. Emphasizing his words with the powerful rock of his hips.

She came again, her body stiffening, her passage tightening in primal spasms. Rafe stilled, groaned, squeezed her hands with his and then relaxed against her. After drawing in a deep breath, he let it out on a moan and lay beside her. *"Claire, Claire, aw, cher. What am I going to do with you?"*

She couldn't move. Could barely think. But he sounded resigned. As if he was done with worrying about her. But he wrapped his arm around her shoulder and she snuggled close and rested her head on his chest.

His skin was hot and damp and his heart still beat double-time beneath her ear. She knew she should get up. She had somewhere to be. Her friend. She needed to save her. Stop her from doing something stupid. But Rafe's rough hand ran up her arm and through her hair, soothing her, caressing her. The tension and terror of the day finally caught up to her. She was exhausted. Her body felt weighted down, so heavy. And her eyes wouldn't stay open....

14

RAFE WAITED UNTIL CLAIRE'S breathing evened out. Until she sighed and burrowed her nose into his ribs. Until his arm fell asleep. Then he slowly slid out from under her, pausing to make sure she didn't stir.

The fact that he wanted to stay in bed and hold her all night was exactly why he had to get up. Nobody had ever been able to sidetrack him like Claire had. And the only thing keeping Claire here was her friend. She would leave him. Her life was a thousand miles from here. Letting himself care about her too much was sheer self-torture. But he wasn't sure how much longer he could be around her and not start to care too deeply. He needed her gone.

So. This would end tonight. One way or another. He'd be damned if he was going to let this problem with Julia go on one more hour. Once he got her away from Armand's influence, she was Claire's problem. And he could get his life back on track.

He stepped into his jeans and tugged a shirt over his head, then grabbed his jacket and gun and silently made his way down to the Barracuda. Before he fired it up, he pulled the magazine from his Sig and emptied the bullets into his palm, then snapped the magazine back in and tossed the bullets in his glove box. The Colony may be a cult of crazies, but they were basically harmless crazies. And he wasn't going to risk shooting anyone, not even for Claire.

His only hesitation was whether to call the cops. There was no crime to report. And if he told them he was going to try to force a woman to leave a cult at gunpoint, he'd be the one they arrested. Even if the gun wasn't loaded.

Grim but determined, he pulled out of the parking lot and headed for the Delacroix Asylum. Shutting off his lights and parking a couple blocks away, he quietly shut his door and began with a reconnaissance outside the house, scouting for alternate escape routes.

When he came upon the only window with a light flickering, he peered inside and, through an opening in the curtains, caught glimpses of people in black hooded robes standing in a circle. There were only about six or seven, so crowd control shouldn't be too tough.

Armand's white-blond hair stood out in the center of the ring. He'd pulled his hood back and was holding up an ornate golden chalice above his head with both hands. Rafe couldn't see Julia at all. Not good.

He returned to the broken window he'd found on the

other side of the house and cautiously climbed through, landing awkwardly on broken floorboards. He lost his balance and fell, knocking against a pile of old, smashed chairs. They toppled over with a loud crash and Rafe froze, his heart hammering against his ribs. He could only hope the chanting he heard in the distance had covered up the sound.

After a few tension-filled moments, he took a cautious step and the creaking wood made his pulse jump. From then on, he took every step painstakingly slowly until he finally made his way to the ceremony room.

Not knowing what to expect, he pulled his Sig before stepping through the door. For a moment he wished he'd kept it loaded. But no one even noticed him. He made his way inside the room and aimed the gun at the circle of robes. "Everyone stay calm and do what I say and no one gets hurt."

The chanting stopped. The circle broke and one of the female cult members screamed and scattered for the door. A couple more spun toward him in surprise and then backed away from him with their hands raised. The rest merely turned to stare.

As they moved he saw Julia on her knees before Armand. She wore the same black robe, but it was open down the front and she was nude underneath. A trickle of blood ran from two cuts down the side of her neck onto her collarbone. She was holding the chalice and it was almost to her lips.

Armand's face contorted with rage. "How dare you interrupt our sacred ceremony?"

Rafe aimed the Sig at him. "Yeah, it's a crying shame. Julia, get up and come with me or your boyfriend gets it." He sure hoped she believed he would actually shoot someone. Otherwise he was out of options.

Julia's gaze darted back and forth between Rafe and Armand, fear and confusion apparent in her expression. She rose to her feet and started toward Rafe. Armand grabbed her arms and held her in front of him. "My blood bride and I are immortal. Your bullets cannot hurt us." Still with the fake French accent.

Julia frowned. "But my love, I haven't drunk your blood yet."

"He will not shoot you, beloved. You must trust me."

"You willing to risk your life for this guy, Julia?" Rafe cocked the gun.

Julia blinked. Rafe could see the cogs turning in her mind. Would she figure out the flaw in this con man's logic? Her eyes narrowed and she tilted her head. "But…if you're immortal, then you should be guarding me, right?"

Armand smiled and bent over to speak softly in her ear. "Julia, my life's blood. This is a test. You must be willing to die for me. And then I will make you immortal."

Rafe laughed. And if she believed that one… Julia frowned, obviously torn. She turned to face Rafe. "Why are you doing this?"

The circle of followers turned from Armand to Rafe also, watching events as if this was a stage play and they were the audience.

Rafe shrugged, still aiming the gun at Armand, his left hand supporting his right. "Claire refuses to leave New Orleans without you."

She frowned. "She's still here? But why?"

"She told me all about how you saved her when you were kids, and how she would never have had the courage to go on to become who she is without you. She'll never give up on you, Julia."

Tears welled up in Julia's eyes and spilled down her cheeks. She sniffed and wiped her eyes on her sleeve. "She told you all that? That *I* gave *her* courage?"

"Julia, don't listen to him, my beloved." Armand put his arm around her shoulders, but she shrugged him off.

Her gaze moved past Rafe, her eyes widened and she pointed above his shoulder. "Look out!"

Rafe dodged right and the two-by-four meant for his head hit his shoulders. The force of the blow knocked him to his knees and he dropped the gun. It spun across the floor somewhere to his right. He didn't have time to look. He was too busy fending off another blow from the wooden beam.

When his attacker swung again, Rafe rolled to his back and caught the blow with his forearm. He thought he heard a bone crack and excruciating pain shot up his left arm. With a grunt, he kicked out and caught

Shadow in the shin, kicked again and the guy dropped to his knees.

Rafe jumped him, knocking him onto his back and then planted his fist in the guy's face. While he was still stunned from the first punch, Rafe pulled back and hit him again. Rafe felt the satisfying crunch of broken cartilage and blood splattered from Shadow's nose.

But Shadow grabbed Rafe's broken left arm and wrenched it behind him. Rafe yelled out in pain and Shadow scrambled away.

Rafe tried to chase him, but Shadow got to the gun first.

Shadow grabbed it and pointed it at Rafe, then swung it around to aim at Armand. "Nobody move!"

The other cult followers let out a collective gasp.

Armand held tight to Julia.

Shadow's body twitched. He was sweating and sniffing and wiping his temple on his shoulder. He waved the Sig around wildly. "I want the money!"

Rafe's arm throbbed. He held it to his side, waiting to see what Shadow would do.

Nobody else responded. But Rafe noticed Armand's gaze darted to a crumbling fireplace on the wall to his left.

"I said I want the money and I want it now!" Shadow staggered over to Armand and held the gun to his head. "And I want Julia back. You stole her from me!"

"Here, take her!" Armand's French accent had disappeared as he shoved Julia into Shadow.

"Armand!" Julia looked repulsed and disillusioned at the same time. But Shadow had his arm tight around her neck as he turned the gun on her. "You gotta help me find the money, baby. I need it, okay?

"Sweetie, I don't know about any money. Armand? What's he talking about?"

"I don't know, I swear. He's crazy."

She narrowed her eyes. "You lost your accent, *beloved*."

Rafe had to give her credit. Julia was playing it pretty cool.

Shadow spat. "He drugs you, see? A-and then he gets you to sign over your money to him."

Julia gasped. "You bastard!" She struggled against Shadow, trying to get to Armand, presumably to claw his eyes out, and Shadow used the hand holding the gun to restrain her arm.

Rafe wouldn't get a better chance. He charged him, punched him in the temple.

The gun went flying as Shadow staggered back. But he recovered quickly and charged Rafe, knocking him down. Shadow fought like a crazed man, rolling on top of Rafe and wrapping his hands around his neck, choking him. Rafe punched his jaw and reared back for another shot when the light was blocked by a figure and a two-by-four came smashing down on the back of Shadow's head.

Shadow dropped on top of Rafe, out cold. Rafe shoved him off and sat up.

She stood over him wielding the piece of wood like an avenging angel come to save the innocent. "Claire?"

"WHAT THE HELL DO YOU think you're doing?" Rafe snarled at her.

She blinked behind her thick glasses. "Saving you."

"I didn't need saving." He gingerly got to his feet, ignoring the hand she offered. "I had it under control."

Fists on hips, she raised her brows. "I'll remember that next time."

Favoring his left arm, he found his Sig and bent to retrieve it, and she caught him wincing.

"You're hurt!" She marched over to him and tried to examine his arm. It was swollen and already turning purple.

He pulled away from her. "I'm fine."

Yeah, right. Blood ran from a cut lip. His cheek was reddened and his right eye was swollen. Of all the stubborn, prideful, male ego—

"Claire?" Julia rushed to her and hugged her.

"Julia!" Claire slowly lifted her arms around Claire and returned the hug.

Julia started sobbing. "I'm so sorry. You were right. Armand was nothing but a fake and a liar. Why do I always get mixed up with these losers?"

"Shh, it's all right." Claire patted her back awkwardly.

"I want to go home," Julia wailed. "Can we just go home now?"

"Yes. We will. It's all over now. Let's get out of this strange city and go home." Why did that sound like the very last thing she wanted to do? But she couldn't stay in New Orleans. Her life was in Boston. Her job. Her...coworkers.

Julia pulled away and gripped the front of her robe together. "I don't ever want to do Mardi Gras again."

Claire examined the cuts on Julia's neck. "These might need stitches. We need to get you to the hospital."

Julia gave her a wobbly smile. "Okay." Then she scowled. "Wait a minute." She twisted around to scan the room. "Where's Armand?"

The few followers left standing around looked around the room also. No Armand.

And Rafe was missing, too.

Then a high-pitched wail came from the front part of the house.

Claire rushed out, followed by Julia and the rest of The Colony.

By the time they reached the entryway, Rafe was holding the gun on Armand with a satisfied smirk on his face. Armand was on his knees holding up a black duffle bag bulging at the seams.

"Take it," Armand cried. "Just don't shoot me."

"Toss it over to the ladies," Rafe ordered, gesturing to Claire with the gun.

Armand pitched it toward them, and then stuck his hands above his head.

Julia dove for the bag and unzipped it, the other followers gathering around her.

Julia shrieked. "He must have hundreds of thousands in here." She started pulling out wads of cash. The other followers swarmed the bag, demanding their money back. "Just hold on." Julia held the bag against her chest. "If he got to all our bank accounts, we'll all have to check our statements online and see who is owed what. I say we give the bag to the police as evidence so they can arrest this scumbag and put him away for a long time. Deal?"

The others grumbled and a few complained as Julia stood and handed the bag to Claire.

"What's your real name?" Rafe asked Armand.

"I-it's Jed. Jed Banks." No trace of a French accent now.

"Claire, call the cops and tell them we have a thief they might want to come arrest named Jed Banks. He's probably got priors."

Jed whined. "Come on. Everybody got their money back, didn't they?"

Claire ignored the thieving coward and called Sergeant Mulroney. Again, though it was after midnight, he answered. She explained the whole situation and gave him their location. He told her he'd send several squad cars out and then hung up.

She moved to stand beside Rafe, even though his right arm never wavered holding the gun, his left arm hung useless at his side. Pain etched lines around his mouth. She'd never admired a man more. "What now?"

Rafe called to The Colony people. "You think you can keep your fake guru from getting away until the cops get here?"

Several of the black-robed figures came forward and took hold of Jed by his arms. Jed began pleading with them to let him go. That he hadn't harmed anyone.

Rafe dropped his right arm, turned and headed for the front door.

Claire followed him and caught up. "I'm taking you and Julia to the hospital." She held out her palm. "Give me your keys."

Rafe halted on the front porch. "Like hell," he ground between his teeth.

Claire stopped abruptly. "Rafe. Be reasonable. You can't drive with a broken arm."

"Can you drive a stick?"

"Uh…I understand the basic mechanics involved."

"That's what I thought."

"I can drive a manual transmission." Julia piped up from behind them. "My car's a five-speed."

"You should both wait here for the police."

Claire shook her head. "So should you."

He grimaced. "Cops and I don't generally see eye to eye on things. They might not appreciate the fact that I used this." He held up the gun.

"About that." Julia folded her arms. "Would you really have shot me?"

"Hold out your hand," he ordered Julia.

She did and he pressed something on the gun and a long black metal piece fell out and into her palm.

"Check inside the magazine," he said.

Julia looked surprised. "It's empty."

"What?" Claire wanted to throttle him. "You came here and faced a cult with an unloaded gun? Of all the stupid, dangerous stunts! What if—"

"Claire?" Julia cut her off.

"What?" she snapped.

"We should probably get him to the hospital."

Claire frowned. "Fine." She turned to Rafe. "Julia drives."

For a moment he looked as if he might argue, but he finally gave a disgusted sigh and pulled his keys from the pocket of his leather jacket. "I can't believe I'm letting the cracked chick drive my car."

Julia grinned and took the keys and they fell into step together down the porch steps. Claire stopped and watched them head down the circular drive.

"You realize this is a classic car, right?" she heard Rafe telling Julia. "It's irreplaceable."

"What kind is it?"

"A seventy-three Barracuda."

"Oooh, I love those big strong muscle cars. 340? Four speed?"

Rafe's jaw dropped.

Claire blinked back tears. It was over. Julia was going to be all right. And Rafe. He'd risked his life for her. How did you repay someone for that? Just saying thank you seemed embarrassingly inadequate.

But saying goodbye was going to be even harder.

15

CLAIRE WORRIED HER thumbnail and tried to stay calm as she sat in the emergency room. She hated feeling so useless. She could tell Rafe was in pain, yet he sat stoically, refusing even an aspirin.

Cell generation was all about the future of human health. But working in a lab all day, looking into microscopes and running tests was nothing like the chaos and the suffering of life in the trenches of emergency health care. This trip had certainly yanked the blinders from her eyes and made her see how insulated she was in her own safe little world.

Rafe was finally taken back to a treatment room. And after waiting another hour amid the groans and whispers of the sick and injured, Julia was finally called to a room. Claire went with her.

The physician's assistant examining Julia stated she didn't need stitches. She applied butterfly bandages, asked her about a tetanus shot and then discharged her.

The P.A. didn't act surprised to see someone come in wearing nothing but a black hooded robe and sporting two puncture wounds on her neck.

That was somehow more disturbing than Julia's non-chalance about her wounds.

"Really, Claire, they're no big deal." Julia flashed her winning smile. "The scars will only make the story better when I tell it at work." She signed the papers the nurse brought her for discharge and then hopped off the examination table and peeked through the privacy curtain. "Honestly, have you seen all the hot doctors in this place? Mmm, maybe I should get hurt more often."

Claire took off her glasses and pinched the bridge of her nose. It was either that or smack Julia upside the head. She was already looking for another man.

The only man Claire could think about right now was Rafe. He'd gone off with a different nurse to a separate treatment room and she hadn't seen him since. That had been two hours ago.

Was his arm broken? Had they set it? Was he in pain? She slipped her glasses back on and then chewed on her thumbnail.

What if she never saw him again? A sharp ache stabbed her chest. Never see that roguish grin or those steel-gray eyes? Never feel his rough hands on her skin or hear that soft southern voice? She took off her glasses again, wiped her eyes and then put them back on.

"Hey, what's the matter?" Julia hunkered down in front of her and held her shoulders.

"Nothing." She straightened her spine and managed to meet Julia's gaze and smile. "I'm just tired."

"Guess you can't wait to get back to your normal routine, huh? I'm so sorry I've caused you all this trouble. I don't know what I was thinking!" She curled her hand into the shape of a gun and pretended to shoot herself in the head. "I've learned my lesson, though, I swear." She leaned forward and wrapped Claire in a big hug. "I'm really sorry I said those things. I didn't mean them."

"I know you didn't. But in all fairness, I think some of it is true. I do tend to be…rigid in my routine."

Julia sat back on her heels. "But that's just who you are, Claire. I shouldn't try to change you. Believe me, I could learn a lesson from you about responsibility."

Claire smiled. "Tell you what. I'll try to be more spontaneous. And you try to be more responsible."

Julia stuck out her right hand. "Deal."

"So, do you want to get out of here?"

"Let's go." Julia got to her feet and headed out of the room and down the corridor. She'd gone about three feet when she stopped in her tracks. "What about your boyfriend?"

"He's not my boyfriend."

Julia grinned. "If he's not your boyfriend, then why do you keep making googly eyes at him?"

Claire blinked. "I do not— Never mind."

"What was his name again? Rafe? I love that name. I bet it's short for Rafael. Oh, Rafe?" she yelled down the length of the corridor. "Which room are you in?"

"Julia!" Claire whispered loudly and made a grab for her arm.

Julia pulled away. "Oh, Rafe," she singsonged, peeking into a door that was half-open.

Claire hurried to catch up to her. "Julia, you're infringing on people's privacy. We can wait for him in the lobby."

A door on her right opened and Rafe stepped out into the hallway not two feet from where she stood.

Claire sucked in a breath. He was disheveled, unshaven, deliciously rumpled. He wore only his lowslung jeans. His left arm was in a cast and held with a sling against his chest. His very bare chest. All that onze skin and hard muscle. She licked her lips. He ed heat and she wanted to rub up against him and

 love your tat. What is it?" Julia asked. She over Rafe from head to toe and Claire a strong impulse to step in front of the e!"

hest and then back to meet Ju-
ans Risen from the Dead."
e'd told her of his parents
nd it hit her, vampires
 Rafe had been ex-
rrifically up-close-
attoos were his way of

She wanted to hug him and hold him and comfort him the way he'd comforted her after rescuing her from the tomb. She wanted to drag him back inside that treatment room and push him down onto the examining table and crawl up and over him and unbutton his jeans—

"Excuse me."

Claire snapped out of her fantasy. A nurse wheeling a hospital bed transporting an elderly lady stood in front of her. What was she doing? Blocking an emergency room hallway while daydreaming about a sexual encounter? What was wrong with her?

"I'm s-sorry." She sidestepped out of the way and the nurse wheeled the bed past her. Rafe stood next to her. She could feel him looking at her, but she couldn't meet his gaze. The spell had been broken. She closed her eyes and bit her lip. If she tried to speak she'd stutter again.

"Ready to go?"

Without thinking, Claire looked at him and g caught in his eyes. "Yes," she breathed.

He nodded and disappeared into the room.

She glanced at Julia. "Would you please bri car up to the doors?"

Julia nodded and winked, and strode off.

After a couple of minutes Rafe reappeared. he had his boots on and one arm in the sl black leather jacket, the other side just dra shoulder. She didn't think it possible a mo he looked even sexier now.

He checked himself. "They had to cut my T-shirt off."

Oh. She'd been staring at his chest again. Her cheeks burned.

He turned and made his way down the maze of corridors to the exit. Claire trailed behind.

Julia sat in the driveway waiting at the wheel. He held the door and folded the front passenger seat up for Claire. She climbed into the back, her knees almost to her chin.

"I'll say this for New Orleans—no shortage of sexy men down here." Julia wiggled her brows as Rafe got in.

Rafe gave her a lopsided smile and verbal directions to his place, and Julia headed out of the hospital parking lot, chattering away.

He took Julia's flirting in stride, no doubt accustomed to women falling all over him. Before Claire. And after.

Why was she feeling so possessive? He wasn't hers. She wasn't his. And she could list a dozen reasons why they never would be. Yes, a list. That's what she should do. She'd make a mental list. To remind herself why she was returning to Boston.

One: Rafe was a consummate player. What had Rowena called him? The King of Flings.

Two: Her home and her job were more than thirteen hundred miles away.

Three: She had only known the man six days. Not even that. No rational person could fall in love with someone in such a short length of time. Relationships took months—years sometimes—to develop. Theirs was merely a bond forged during an intense situation. It couldn't last.

"So, Rafe." Julia shifted gears and sped up onto the highway. "How did you know Armand wasn't who he said he was?"

Yeah. How *had* he known?

Rafe shrugged. "I've known plenty of guys like him. Con artist. Chooses his marks well, lonely, needy—no offense—" He glanced at Julia.

"Hey, if the shoe fits me…"

"Anyway, he convinces them to hand over their 'worldly' possessions, including bank accounts, and then skips town before anyone fingers him as a fraud."

Julia shook her head. "I got so sucked into his head game. I really thought he loved me." Her voice wobbled on the last word.

Claire leaned forward, put her hand on Julia's shoulder. "Do you think he got access to your bank account?"

Julia sniffed, and then shrugged. "I'll have to check." She twisted to glance at Claire and flashed her famous mischievous grin. "But I want to go to the police and press charges after we drop Rafe off."

She saw Rafe stiffen. Right. They'd be dropping him off, and he'd go back to his life and she'd go back to hers. Claire sat back, studying the fringe on her poncho and trying to ignore the lump in her throat.

"Oookaaay," Julia said. "How 'bout them Saints, huh?"

Claire sank farther into the backseat. She should continue her list. Where was she?

Four: Rafe was all wrong for her. She needed someone steady, reliable, normal. Geez, that sounded mind-numbing. And from the moment she'd asked him to help her, Rafe had been reliable, hadn't he? He owned his own business. A person didn't get much steadier than that.

Wait. This was supposed to be her list of reasons why they would never work. She chewed her thumbnail.

Julia exited the freeway and stopped at an intersection. "Which way?"

"Left." Rafe was staring out the window.

They weren't far from Once Bitten. Claire used her cell to call the cab company she'd been using, and asked them to pick her up outside the bar. She noticed Rafe's jaw muscle twitch, but he didn't say anything. Did he not want her to go? He'd asked her to stay one more day yesterday morning. Did he still feel that way?

If he did, he didn't say anything.

Silence had never felt so awkward. Claire tried to think of number five and gave up. The list seemed silly now. And pointless.

Before she could accept that it was really over, Julia had pulled into the parking lot behind Once Bitten, and she and Rafe were climbing out of the car and shaking hands goodbye.

Then Rafe turned to her. Claire stared at him. It was the middle of the night. It was cold and all he had on was his jacket draped over one shoulder. He should be freezing. But she could feel the heat radiating from him.

Julia cleared her throat. "Well, I'll…wait for the cab over there." She pointed vaguely toward the street and then tossed Rafe his keys.

He caught them without looking her way.

Claire swallowed. Her chest felt as if it'd been invaded by flesh-eating microorganisms. She hitched her purse higher on her shoulder and extended her right hand, then withdrew it. She remembered how he'd mockingly kissed the back of it last time she'd done that.

"Well, *cher.*" A corner of his mouth turned up. "It's been…interesting." He stepped close, crooked a finger under her chin and lifted her face to his. "You have a safe flight back to Boston, now, you hear?" He lowered his head and touched his lips to hers.

She opened her mouth and leaned into him, but he lifted his head and stepped back. His gray eyes were the color of the ocean during a crackling storm, and just as turbulent.

She bit her bottom lip to keep it from trembling. Hard to believe she'd never see him again. Hard to believe that thought could hurt so much after knowing him less than a week. She wanted to say something important. Something profound. *Something.* At the very least she could tell him how grateful she was for all he'd done for her.

She drew in a deep breath. "Goodbye, Rafe."

As she got in the cab and it pulled away, she turned to stare out the back windshield.

He was still there, watching her.

AFTER THE CAB PULLED AWAY Rafe clenched his fists and finally let himself into the bar.

Usually at this time of night—or rather, early morning, the bar would be hitting its stride. The music would be blaring, the crowd would be calling for more beers and he'd be making a date with some hot chick for later.

Tonight it was silent. Empty. Dead.

And he was alone.

He'd feel better tomorrow night. Once the bar was open, and the music was blaring and the lights were on and people were lined up to get in. This bar was his dream. His life. He didn't need anything else.

Except a new assistant manager.

And maybe a quirky brunette to seduce every night.

Whoa. Every night?

Claire had mentioned she wouldn't be pressing charges against Ro. She still could, he supposed. He wouldn't blame her. Even now when he thought about how upset and vulnerable she'd been after he let her out of that tomb he wanted to smash something. She'd felt so good in his arms. He'd liked being the good guy for once. Liked the glow of admiration in her eyes after he stopped Banks from making off with all that cash. He'd felt more alive in that moment, hell, in the past week with Claire, than he'd ever felt. More a part of something bigger, more…important.

He wandered behind the bar, gazed out at the only thing he'd ever thought he wanted. And it seemed…not enough anymore.

And what did he think he could do about it? If he called Claire up right now and asked her to stay, she'd think he'd lost his mind. Her life was back in Boston. She barely knew him.

And what would they do, even if she lived here? Did he really think he could sustain a relationship for longer than twelve hours?

Damn it. He grabbed a bottle of Wild Turkey and a tumbler and splashed the amber liquid up to the brim.

16

"CLAIRE!" FINGERS SNAPPED an inch from Claire's nose.

Claire blinked and brought her attention back to Julia.

The past few hours Claire had felt as if she were wandering around in a soupy fog.

Julia had taken charge, as she usually did when the two of them were together. Except where normally Claire would've worried about the arrangements and double-checked the details unbeknownst to Julia, she didn't. It didn't seem to matter.

After the cab dropped them at the police station, they'd spent a couple of hours filing the charges against Jed Banks, giving a detective separate detailed accounts of the events at the asylum tonight before they were finally allowed to leave.

The detective had a squad car deliver them to the Les Chambres Royale and asked them to stay in touch.

That was more than Rafe had done. Claire tried to put that thought out of her mind.

As Claire retrieved her luggage from the concierge, Julia turned to her. Did she want to get a room and shower and sleep for the rest of the night and find a flight later today?

Claire shrugged. She'd been in the same outfit for two days, but she didn't care. Whatever Julia wanted to do.

Julia asked the concierge to check flights to Missouri and Boston. There was a charge to change the dates on their return tickets, but both cities had flights departing around 7:00 a.m. They could just go to the airport and get some breakfast there, Julia suggested. Get the heck out of this city.

Claire nodded. If that was what Julia wanted to do, that was fine. Why was Julia acting all exasperated?

"Hello? Earth to Claire." Julia waved a hand.

"What?" Claire snapped. "Just do whatever you want. I honestly don't care."

Julia's eyes bulged. "Do you hear yourself? What is going on?"

She took her glasses off and rubbed her eyes. "I guess I'm just tired. Let's get a room and leave tomorrow. What's one more day?" She slipped her glasses back on and headed for the registration desk.

Julia grabbed her arm. "Hold on. You don't feel the urgent need to get back to work as soon as possible?

After you've been gone almost a week longer than you planned? Isn't your boss going to be upset?"

"Oh, Beckley can go suck a lemon."

"Oh. My. God." Julia kept hold of her arm and led her to a comfy seating area off the main lobby. Julia pushed down on her shoulders till she sat and then pulled up an ottoman to sit directly in front of her.

Claire met Julia's questioning gaze. But she had no answer. She shook her head. She shrugged. And all of a sudden tears welled in her eyes. No. She couldn't be crying. Not again. She never cried. In twenty-nine years she could probably count the number of times she'd cried on one hand before this week. And they had all been before she'd turned ten.

"Oh, Claire." Julia wrapped her arms around her and Claire lost whatever control she'd had. Tears spilled down her cheeks. "Okay, let's get a room. You need a hot shower, some breakfast and a long sleep, I think."

She stood and walked briskly to the registration desk and came back within minutes, gathered Claire up and walked her to the elevator.

She took care of their luggage, pushed Claire into the bathroom after starting the shower running and by the time Claire stepped out of the steaming bathroom, a tray from room service waited on the table.

Numb, Claire ate, and then crawled into the double bed closest to the window. But her eyes wouldn't close. When she rolled over, Julia was sleeping like the proverbial log. She felt the inexplicable depression settling over her again.

She grabbed her glasses off the side table and sat up. Distraction. That's what she needed. She found the remote and turned on the television. Infomercial. *Click.* Infomercial. *Click.* Cartoons. *Click.* Ah, a movie. The hero had his left arm in a sling with only one arm in his jacket. Just as Rafe had. The heroine was telling him goodbye and boarding a plane. The plane started to take off. Through the window, she watched him standing there.

Then the heroine called out to the pilot to stop the plane. As it screeched to a halt she bolted out and ran into the hero's arms. Even one-armed, he held her so tight, and as the music swelled they kissed with such passion it made Claire's stomach ache. But they could never be together. Their worlds were too different.

Claire lost it. She pulled a pillow to her face and cried and cried. At least the singer had kissed him goodbye and told she loved him. At least she'd had a moment of truth before returning to her lonely apartment in Boston and her coworkers she barely spoke to, and the excitement of ordering Chinese takeout every Saturday night and eating alone— Wait. She wasn't thinking about the heroine anymore. She was picturing herself running back to that vampire bar and throwing herself into Rafe's arms.

She clicked the TV off, lay back against the headboard and tried to picture herself actually doing that.

Not as the actress in the movie, but in real life. She tried to picture what Rafe would do.

Then she squeezed her eyes closed.

He wouldn't catch her in his arms and kiss her as if tomorrow was the apocalypse. He'd laugh her out of the bar.

No. He'd be nice about it. And that would be worse. He'd give her a look that was the equivalent of a pat on the head and gently push her away. *Love me?* he'd say. *You're just grateful I helped you save your friend.*

Was that all these feelings were? Gratitude?

It had to be. Now that the excitement of the past several days was over, it was only natural there might be some sort of emotional letdown. Right? She took her glasses off and forced herself to concentrate on relaxing her body.

It seemed she'd just closed her eyes when someone jostled her awake. "Claire. Come on, sleepyhead. I booked us flights and they leave in three hours."

Claire opened her eyes and sat up.

Julia yanked open the curtains and bright sunlight blazed into the room. Claire moaned and squinted, reaching for her glasses.

Shoving down all the nonsense of last night, she dressed and packed, and checked out and got in a cab and checked in at the airport. Julia chattered most of the way, which was normal. Claire was always the quiet one in the friendship. And it helped her to keep ignoring the tumor of irrational emotion that seemed to be growing no matter how determined she was to push it down, deep down.

The airline attendant checked their boarding passes and they settled down to wait for their flights to be called. Claire stared out the bank of terminal windows, unseeing as she listened to Julia talk about coloring her hair red.

Her stomach hurt. She dug in her purse for an antacid or an aspirin. Anything. Her fingers touched Julia's pendant necklace and she pulled it out, thinking she'd give it back to her.

As she looked up, her eyes focused on the windows and beyond them to a plane taking off down the runway. She shot to her feet and spun to Julia. "Here." She extended the necklace dangling from her fingers.

Julia gasped. "My necklace! How'd you get it? After I woke up from spending the night with Shadow, I realized it was gone and that he'd probably stolen it. I was too ashamed to tell you." She took it and clasped it around her neck.

"Sheer luck. A long story. Listen." Claire grabbed her suitcase and overnight bag. Everything she'd been shoving down came boiling up and if she didn't do something she was going to burst.

"What are you doing?"

"Listen, Julia. I—I can't leave yet. I may make a complete fool of myself, but I have to try, you know? Otherwise I'll—"

Julia squealed and jumped up to capture Claire in her arms. "Yes! Go! I was so hoping there was something between you and Rafe."

"You were?"

"Oh, Claire. If you'd only seen the way you two looked at each other." Julia was shaking her head, her lips pursed. "Puhlease."

"Rafe was? I mean, looking at me?"

"Well, I guess I'm not the best judge of these things. I mean, I thought Armand loved me, didn't I?" She peered off into the distance and scrunched up her face and then snapped her gaze back to Claire. "But that's not important." She waved her hand.

"It's not?" Claire was losing her courage.

"No. It's not," Julia insisted. "What's important is that you find out. Right?"

"Right." Claire nodded. "Find out what?" She just wanted to be sure what Julia was saying made sense because right now everything was starting to seem surreal.

"If he loves you like he looked like he loved you last night." Julia took hold of Claire's shoulders, spun her to face the exit and pushed. "Now go! I'll get our tickets changed to later flights and catch a cab to the hotel."

Claire glanced back. "You're not going home?"

"Are you kidding?" Julia grinned. "I have to see how this all turns out. Call me, okay?"

Claire nodded and started walking toward the exit. Walking accelerated to jogging. And jogging turned to running.

RAFE WOKE UP AS HIS head hit the floor. He groaned and lay still until the dizziness passed. Then he opened one bleary eye.

He was in his office. There was bright afternoon light slanting in through the blinds. He'd fallen off the sofa.

He closed his eyes and pressed his palms over them and rubbed. Or one palm, anyway. The other was half-covered in a cast.

Now he remembered. He'd taken the bottle of Wild Turkey—but not the tumbler—with him to his office last night, or early this morning, actually. He must've passed out.

Disgusted, he tried to sit up and pain shot through his head. His stomach was traveling on a fishing boat in choppy waters. He lay still until the queasiness subsided and then tried again. Water. Aspirin. He made it to the sink behind the bar and nearly spilled the aspirin trying to get the cap off with one hand. He had to slump down on a stool before he could swallow the medicine and toss back the glass of water.

He looked at himself in the mirror behind the bar and scowled. How had he let himself get like this? His gaze landed on the beer clock. Only an hour until he was supposed to open?

He shot off the stool and bolted up the stairs to his apartment, someone hammering wooden stakes into his head. He needed a hot shower, a thorough teeth brushing and a shave. All of which would take twice as long to complete with his arm in a cast. Mixing drinks with one hand was going to be a pain in the butt, too.

As he entered his apartment, he looked at it as if seeing it for the first time. Shabby, tiny, messy. The only thing of any quality was the bed. And the sheets were rumpled, the comforter lying in a heap on the floor. He found himself bending over the side where Claire had laid and inhaling. Yes. Just a hint of her scent, a clean, laundry detergent type of smell, but mixed with honey.

He closed his eyes and inhaled again, and saw her lying in his bed. Now he really was torturing himself. He ran a hand over the sheets and saw her long legs, her voluptuous breasts and her big brown eyes staring at him in wonder, as if he'd just reached up and plucked the moon from the sky and handed it to her on a silver platter.

No one had ever looked at him like that before. Just like no one had ever had his back in a fight before. He couldn't believe she'd shown up and whacked Shadow over the head like that. He knew she couldn't possibly be accustomed to such physical violence. And yet she'd said she was saving him.

Saving him…

His gut twisted and this time he didn't think it had anything to do with a hangover.

He got cleaned up with barely a minute to spare and went downstairs to switch on the lights and music. Bulldog and his two waitresses were waiting as he unlocked the front door, as well as a fairly long line of goth and vampire-costumed customers.

Closing the bar last night didn't seem to have hurt business. He took his place behind the bar and signaled to Bulldog to let 'em in. And he got busy filling orders. Draft beers, mixed drinks, the hard stuff on the rocks or neat.

Along with the regulars on stools were plenty of tourists in street clothes. Middle-aged couples wanting to add a little spice to their routine lives, Sorority girls looking for a hook-up and—Rafe froze. He blinked. Standing at the bar where he'd first seen her was a tall geeky-looking woman wearing thick glasses and a multi-colored knitted monstrosity with fringe. A riot of brunette curls framed her face.

He just stood and stared at her.

She met his gaze and the passion in her eyes made his chest expand with something like joy. Yeah, he was pretty sure this was joy he was feeling.

He sauntered over and leaned his right palm on the bar. "What can I do for you, *cher?*"

She bit her beautiful bottom lip and pushed her glasses up her nose. "I, uh…" She cleared her throat. She was adorable. He leaned over the bar, cupped her face with his good hand and kissed her.

With a whimper, she threw her arms around his neck and opened to him, deepening the kiss. Vaguely he noticed gasps and murmurs and whistles from the crowd, but all he could feel was Claire. In his arms, the taste of her, the scent.

"Come here." He slid his hand around her waist and lifted and pulled and she hopped and landed her butt on the bar. In a denim skirt and half boots, she swung her legs over and slid down on his side and into his arms. Screw the sling, he needed to hold her.

Ignoring the complaints and grumbling from customers, he stared into her eyes. "This isn't a goodbye kiss, I hope. 'Cause I'm not letting you go now. You're caught in my vampire's lair."

She raised her brows, but her mouth was turned up at the corners. "Are you hypnotizing me to your will?"

He slowly moved her hair away from the tender part of her neck, sank his mouth onto the flesh, scraped his teeth and then kissed all along the curve of her neck. "Is it working?"

She dropped her head back and moaned. "Yes."

He grinned. "Good." He cupped the back of her head and covered her lips with his. With the kiss he tried to convey all the emotions he could barely name much less speak. Joy and hope. And love— Well, he should probably say that in a minute. He slanted his mouth over hers and poured his soul into the kiss.

"I love you." He trailed tiny kisses from the corner of her mouth to her jaw. "I want you to stay." More kisses along her delicate ear to her temple. "For as long as you can." He kissed her eyes. "I don't know how—"

"It doesn't matter." She kissed him back, running her

fingers over his scruffy cheeks and through his hair. "We'll work something out later. I don't need a plan right now. I just need you."

He hugged her close and kissed her deep and wet until he couldn't tell who was kissing who.

He pulled back, narrowed his eyes. "Don't you want to spout some statistic about the survival rate of relationships that begin with a dangerous experience?"

She smiled and chuckled. He'd never heard her laugh. It was rich and throaty, sexy as hell. "Screw statistics." She pushed the hair from his eyes. "I love you, Rafe Moreau."

Epilogue

1 year later—Mardi Gras

CLAIRE HESITATED AT THE door to Once Bitten, tugging up her black hose and tugging down the hem of her short black dress. She smoothed her hair, pulled up and back, the frizzy curls tamed into shiny ringlets that hung from a topknot. The style was Julia's suggestion. She'd said it resembled a witch's hairdo from an old vampire soap opera.

Resisting the urge to check her makeup one more time, Claire took a deep breath, licked her bloodred lips and swung open the door.

The bar was full to capacity. There were the usual Goths and vamps. The mostly naked snake lady, the girls dancing in the hanging cages. And tonight there were swarms of tourists looking to party hard.

The season of Carnival had begun two weeks ago, with several parades each day marching uptown and through mid-city. But today was Lundi Gras, and the big parade was rolling its outrageously spectacular floats down St. Charles Avenue tonight. This was the most exciting time of the year in New Orleans, and Claire's favorite. Of course, she had other, more personal reasons for that.

She scanned behind the bar for Rafe, spotting him instantly in the sexy, gray button-down she'd bought him for his birthday last month. She'd told him it brought out the silver of his eyes and he'd gotten so quiet, at first, she'd thought he didn't like it. When she asked if she should return it, he'd turned away, grabbed a towel to wipe a glass and admitted, after clearing his throat, that he hadn't had a birthday present since he was a kid.

She'd taken him in her arms and they'd made love right there against the bar.

Now, he was smiling and juggling bottles and mixing drinks with the fluid grace she admired the first time she'd seen him. Her insides tingled just watching him.

As if he felt her stare, he looked up and caught her eye. His smile went slack and his eyes flared. She felt his gaze intensely, as if he were touching her with his skillful hands.

Consumed with love, she smiled and made her way through the crowd toward him.

Rafe placed drinks in front of a couple of tourists and then sauntered over to her. "*Cher,* you gonna make it hard for me to stay behind this bar and work all night."

She pretend pouted and leaned forward over the bar,

knowing the low-cut dress would show even more of her cleavage. "I don't mean to make it hard."

"Yes, you do." His eyes flared. "I could tell Reggie I'm taking a break and haul you upstairs right now," he murmured in a husky voice.

Ooh, how she'd love that. She checked out the tall, intelligent black man at the other end of the bar making drinks as fast as his hands could move, and sighed. "We better wait. Reggie is too good of an assistant manager to lose, and I don't think he would appreciate being left alone when you're this busy."

"You're right. But as soon as I lock the door on the last customer, you better watch out, *cher*." His penetrating eyes seemed to see right into her soul. She hoped he could see how much she loved him.

If anyone had told her a year ago that she'd quit her job, uproot her entire life and move to New Orleans, she'd have thought they were high on something illegal. But she was surprisingly good at her new job, and her little row house had way more character than the sterile apartment she'd rented in Boston. But most of all, she loved the relationship she had with Rafe. They were friends and lovers and she loved who she was when she was with him.

A couple of cute coeds called for frozen margaritas and Rafe glanced their way, and then motioned for Claire to follow him as he began making the drinks. "How'd your classes at Tulane go this morning?"

"I can't believe how much I love teaching. I hope I

can make a difference. Did you know that only twenty-two percent of microbiologist majors are female?"

He raised a brow. "I did not know that." His sizzling gaze dropped to her cleavage. "Long as you didn't teach your classes looking like that." He gave a low growl.

"No, I was just my normal fangtastic self." She flashed her fake fangs at him.

Rafe grimaced and rolled his eyes.

She giggled, noticing the way his lips twitched as he tried not to smile at her corny joke. "So, hand me a tray and let me help out." She gestured to the crowded sofas.

"Seriously, *cher?*" He glanced at her as he filled several more orders for a waitress.

"I think I can manage not to spill drinks on the customers." She snatched up a tray and order pad and headed out, checking with the other waitresses as to where they needed her help.

As she took drink orders, she smiled and asked tourists where they were from. Sometimes she joked and flashed her fangs. Who'd have thought she'd ever have the confidence to do that? But Rafe made her feel beautiful. And sexy. And loved.

She noticed him again and smiled and he winked before returning to his customer. The next time she brought him a drink order, she waited while he filled it. "I wish Julia had been able to fly in today."

Rafe frowned. "Wasn't she supposed to?"

Claire shook her head. "She texted me yesterday

and said her new salon was too busy for her to take time off work."

Rafe scowled. "She's not gonna be happy that she missed this," he mumbled.

"What?"

He looked up quickly with wide-eyed innocence. "Nothing."

After a moment's hesitation, Claire shrugged and turned to deliver her drinks. Collecting the money, she heard shouting from the bar.

When she glanced over, Reggie was straightening from the waist and produced a large yellow, purple and green iced cake complete with shiny plastic beads draped across it. He set it on the bar, and then brought out plates and forks and a large knife and gestured her over.

"What's this for?" Claire exchanged her tray for a plate. Checking out the customers on the nearby stools, she noted that the ones closest to her seemed to be waiting expectantly for her to eat her piece of cake.

"It's a King Cake, *cher,*" Rafe said, taking a slice for himself. "A New Orleans Mardi Gras tradition."

Cautiously, she picked up the fork and took a large bite. It was delicious. Kind of a cross between a Bundt cake and a cinnamon roll. She smiled and Rafe returned her smile, just then her fork hit on something solid. Picking the object out of her cake, she stared at it, and then stared at Rafe. It was a tiny plastic baby.

The people around her whooped and cheered and

nudged her with knowing winks. She tried to smile, but she was confused. She gave Rafe a questioning look.

"Every King Cake has a plastic baby hidden in it," Rafe explained. "The person who gets the baby in their slice must provide the cake next year. And—" he brought out a fake metal tiara "—it means you're Queen for the night."

Reggie added, "Or you might be pregnant soon."

Rafe's gaze heated and traveled down to her stomach.

Swallowing a lump in her throat, Claire imagined herself big-bellied with Rafe's child. A black-haired beauty with silver-gray eyes or a darkly handsome kindergartener charming all the girls with his smile. A sharp ache hit her chest. Just a year ago, she'd figured if love and a family were going to happen they would've already.

Rafe reached for a cardboard box nearby and gave it to her. "Help me toss these out, your Majesty."

Claire opened the box to reveal black-and-red shiny beads and gold doubloons. New Orleanians called them "throws." Rafe held another box and began tossing the contents to the crowd.

Claire followed his example and moved out into the dance floor, flinging beads and doubloons. Excited murmurs started buzzing throughout the bar until most of the crowd was swarming around Claire and Rafe, hands in the air, calling, "Throw me something, Mister!"

Claire heard, "Throw me something, Mistress!" She flung the throws until her box was empty.

"Hey, Claire, think fast."

Rafe had pitched something to her. Was he crazy? Didn't he know her well enough by now to realize she wasn't coordinated enough to catch such things? An object sailed toward her as if in slow motion, and she lifted her hands up, waiting like the geeky kid in the outfield hoping to catch the ball that would give the other team its third strike.

No, no, no— She squeezed her eyes closed and… caught it! Fumbled it. Then clutched it against her chest. With an excited grin, she looked up to find Rafe standing right beside her. She gazed down at the black velvet ring box in her hands. Her mouth fell open. She blinked.

"Open it, *cher.*" His Southern drawl was so tender.

She opened the box and a gold ring with a single square-cut diamond sparkled from its bed of black silk.

"I want you in my life forever, Claire. And I want to do this right. Marry me, make a family with me?"

With tears blurring her vision, she nodded, and fell into his arms. She kissed him.

The crowd cheered and whistled and Rafe broke their kiss and called for free drinks for everyone. The crowd hollered even louder and headed for the bar where Reggie and the waitresses were setting up shots.

Rafe's white teeth flashed in that sexy grin of his. He wrapped his arms around her and kissed her so deep and profound she could feel all his hopes and dreams for their future.

"Ow." He pulled back. "You're going to have to take those off." He gingerly fingered her fangs.

"Oh, I don't know. The better to bite you with, my *cherie amour*." She nuzzled into his neck and scraped her teeth against his skin.

He chuckled. "I've been bitten." He cupped her face and looked deep into her eyes. "By love."

She raised her gaze to the ceiling and groaned. "You're so bad, Moreau." She shook her head. "But—" she smiled and kissed him "—that's just one of the things I love about you."

* * * * *

#735 THE ARRANGEMENT
by Stephanie Bond

Ben Winter and Carrie Cassidy have known each other forever. And they like each other—a lot! But when those feelings start to run deeper, Ben thinks he's doing the right thing when he ends the "Friends with Benefits" arrangement he has with Carrie. After all, he wants more from her than just great sex. It seems like a good plan...until Carrie makes him agree to find his replacement!

#736 YOU'RE STILL THE ONE • *Made in Montana*
by Debbi Rawlins

Reluctant dude-ranch manager Rachel McAllister hasn't seen Matt Gunderson since he left town and broke her teenage heart ten years ago. Now the bull-riding rodeo star is back and she's ready to show him *everything* he missed. All she wants is his body, but if there's one thing Matt learned in the rodeo, it's how to hang on tight.

HB0113CNMENHA

#737 NIGHT DRIVING • *Stop the Wedding!*
by Lori Wilde

Former G.I. Boone Toliver has a new mission: prevent his kid sister's whirlwind wedding in Miami. The challenge: Boone can't fly, so he agrees to a road trip with his ditzy neighbor, Tara Duvall. She's shaking the Montana dust from her boots and leaving it all behind for a new start on Florida's sunny beaches. It's one speed bump after another as they deal with clashing personalities and frustrating obstacles, until romantic pit stops and minor mishaps suddenly start to look a whole lot like destiny.

#738 A SEAL'S SEDUCTION • *Uniformly Hot!*
by Tawny Weber

Admiral's daughter Alexia Pierce had no intention of ever letting another military man in her life, even if he was hot! But that was before she met Blake—and learned all the things a navy SEAL was good for....

REQUEST YOUR FREE BOOKS!
2 FREE NOVELS PLUS 2 FREE GIFTS!

red-hot reads!

YES! Please send me 2 FREE Harlequin® Blaze™ novels and my 2 FREE gifts (gifts are worth about $10). After receiving them, if I don't wish to receive any more books, I can return the shipping statement marked "cancel." If I don't cancel, I will receive 6 brand-new novels every month and be billed just $4.49 per book in the U.S. or $4.96 per book in Canada. That's a savings of at least 14% off the cover price. It's quite a bargain. Shipping and handling is just 50¢ per book in the U.S. and 75¢ per book in Canada.* I understand that accepting the 2 free books and gifts places me under no obligation to buy anything. I can always return a shipment and cancel at any time. Even if I never buy another book, the two free books and gifts are mine to keep forever.

151/351 HDN FVPV

Name _____ (PLEASE PRINT) _____

Address _____ Apt. # _____

City _____ State/Prov. _____ Zip/Postal Code _____

Signature (if under 18, a parent or guardian must sign) _____

Mail to the Harlequin® Reader Service:
IN U.S.A.: P.O. Box 1867, Buffalo, NY 14240-1867
IN CANADA: P.O. Box 609, Fort Erie, Ontario L2A 5X3

Want to try two free books from another line?
Call 1-800-873-8635 or visit www.ReaderService.com.

SPECIAL EXCERPT FROM HARLEQUIN® KISS™

Evangeline is surprised when her past lover turns out to be her fiancé's brother. How will she manage the one she loved and the one she has made a deal with?

Follow her path to love January 22, 2013, with

THE ONE THAT GOT AWAY

by Kelly Hunter

"The trouble with memories like ours," he said roughly, "is that you think you've buried them, dealt with them, right up until they reach up and rip out your throat."

Some memories were like that. But not all. Sometimes memories could be finessed into something slightly more palatable.

"Maybe we could try replacing the bad with something a little less intense," she suggested tentatively. "You could try treating me as your future sister-in-law. We could do polite and civil. We could come to like it that way."

"Watching you hang off my brother's arm doesn't make me feel civilized, Evangeline. It makes me want to break things."

Ah.

"Call off the engagement." He wasn't looking at her. And it wasn't a request. "Turn this mess around."

"We need Max's trust fund money."

"I'll cover Max for the money. I'll buy you out."

"What?" Anger slid through her, hot and biting. She could feel her composure slipping away but there was nothing else for it. Not in the face of the hot mess that was Logan. "No," she said as steadily as she could. "No one's buying me out of anything, least of all MEP. That company is *mine,* just as much as it is Max's. I've put six years into it, eighty-hour weeks of blood, sweat, tears and fears into making it the success it is. Prepping it for bigger opportunities, and one of those opportunities is just around the corner. Why on earth would I let you buy me out?"

He meant to use his big body to intimidate her. Closer, and closer still, until the jacket of his suit brushed the silk of her dress, but he didn't touch her, just let the heat build. His lips had that hard sensual curve about them that had haunted her dreams for years. She couldn't stop staring at them.

She needed to stop staring at them.

"You can't be in my life, Lena. Not even on the periphery. I discovered that the hard way ten years ago. So either you leave willingly…or I make you leave."

Find out what Evangeline decides to do by picking up THE ONE THAT GOT AWAY by Kelly Hunter. Available January 22, 2013, wherever Harlequin books are sold.